SONGS

and

PORTOBELLOS

M. A. McCORMACK

First published in 2015 by
McCormack Press
Cuan na nEán
Ballycar, Newmarket on Fergus
Co. Clare
Ireland

CreateSpace paperback	ISBN: 978 1 911013 03 7
Paperback	ISBN: 978 1 911013 00 6
eBook – mobi format	ISBN: 978 1 911013 01 3
eBook – ePub format	ISBN: 978 1 911013 02 0

Produced by Kazoo Independent Publishing Services
222 Beech Park, Lucan, Co. Dublin
www.kazoopublishing.com

Kazoo Independent Publishing Services is not the publisher of this work. All rights and responsibilities pertaining to this work remain with M. A. McCormack.

Kazoo offers independent authors a full range of publishing services. For further details visit www.kazoopublishing.com

Cover design by designforwriters.com

Printed in the EU

Author's note

As a young teenager I wrote stories about the lives of two youngsters, and this book combines some of these stories into a novel. Songs and Portobellos is a combination of my creativity as a teenager, and whatever writing skills that I have acquired as an adult. I have done my very best to do justice and remain loyal to the stories, and I can only hope that I have achieved this.

In the course of writing the book, I have asked myself the question, "Am I the same person that created these stories and characters almost fifty years ago?" My very simple answer is, no. I believe that with most people, perception and imagination becomes distorted by influences and events over the years, and, as a result, most of us no longer carry that unique creativity that we once had.

My hope for this book is that it may provide some understanding to young readers of the value of their own insight and opinions, and perhaps give you the courage to sing your own song. To older readers, I hope that it may rekindle the imagination and spirit that you once had and may have lost.

— M. A. McCormack

Part 1

Chapter 1

It was London in 1961, and the eight-year-old was being made ready for school. Conor was a skinny boy, with black hair and bright blue eyes that seemed to sparkle in his head. The top floor flat at 248 Kensal Road was home to the boy and his parents, and they were the sole occupants of the building. His Mother and Father were both Irish, and had moved to London after the war to seek work. Ireland was in economic isolation in the forties and fifties, and there was nothing for young Irish people to do but head to England or North America in search of opportunities.

Although their country would appear to have failed them, both parents spoke lovingly of Ireland, in particular his father during the family pilgrimages there each summer. Pat, the boy's father, was a tall man with a shock of wavy red hair and a bristly moustache. May, the mother, was a very pretty and petite woman with dark hair and the same colour blue eyes as the boy. His parents had first met at an Irish club in London, and his father told the boy that having danced with his mother for just a few dances, he simply declared, "When are we going home then?" On their way home that first evening, his Mother and Father had shared a single cup of tea at Euston station, and every evening since they got married, they always shared a cup of tea before going to bed.

Pat and May had worked very hard in difficult times to succeed in London. They had very little formal education, but in spite of this, they managed to get well-paid work. When he first arrived in England, his father had trained as an electrician with British Rail. They both now worked in Askey's biscuit factory, his father as a maintenance electrician, and his mother as a packer. Their Kensal Road flat was next door to Askey's and as a consequence, the sweet smell of ice-cream cones hung in the air constantly.

Conor was one of those eight-year-olds who buzzed with energy, and his eyes always seemed to be filled with excitement and curiosity. He was very popular with young and old alike, and took on every task, no matter how mundane or complex, with huge enthusiasm. Each summer the young boy looked forward with a degree of trepidation to their holidays in Ireland. The source of his trepidation was the effect of Ireland on his father, who seemed to change as soon as they stepped off the boat in Dublin. During each holiday his father's drinking became more frequent, and his pride in the country more passionate.

The summer trips were mostly to the West of Ireland, and centred on County Mayo, which was the place of his father's birth. In the course of each holiday, they visited an endless stream of relatives and local pubs, and their entrances and exits were celebrated with much backslapping and banter. The boy's party piece at each venue was to stand on a chair or table and sing 'Sean South of Garryowen'. Although he did not understand the song, he sang it with great gusto. How it sounded coming from an off-key boy soprano with a cockney accent was far from certain, but it did elicit much cheering and endless bottles of lemonade were placed in front of him at its conclusion.

Occasionally on their holidays, his mother would take him to her home town of Cork by train. The little boy loved the train journey, and watched the green farmlands as they passed by the windows of the carriage. His father never joined them on the visits to Cork, which were much more formal than in Mayo. Plates of sandwiches and fruitcake on best bone china were laid out by the mother's sisters, Dolores and Lily. On the sideboards of his aunts' homes were silver-framed photographs of young priests who were their cousins living in America. Unlike the visits to Mayo there was no drinking involved, but over many cups of tea, the mother spoke in great praise of Pat and how well he was doing, and that young Conor was the best in his class at school. Despite the more sedate nature of the visits to Cork, the boy always got a sense of tension between his mother and her sisters that made him feel uncomfortable.

On this particular morning in London as he was finishing off his cornflakes, the boy could tell that his mother was not in a good mood. Conor loved school and was held in very high regard by his teachers. However, his mother had received a letter from the school principle, Miss McNamara, a few days earlier, requesting that she bring the boy and meet with her today at 2 p.m. Before they headed off, his mother stood before him ready for work in her white uniform and turban. She pulled on her beige raincoat and tightened the belt across her waist. Before she went to work, his mother would always walk him the four hundred or so yards to St Charles School. Conor knew the area very well, all the way from Kensal Road to Ladbroke Grove tube station, but he had not as yet been allowed to see himself to school. On this morning he had on his grey school uniform, complete with cap and navy gabardine raincoat. After some adjustments to shoelaces and tie, the boy and his mother made their way down the stairs and out into the hallway.

As they were walking, his mother asked him, "Why does Miss McNamara want to see me? Have you been up to mischief?"

The boy stopped and looked at her. "No, I don't think so."

"Are you sure, Conor?" she said sharply.

He nodded his head and said, "Yes."

Outside on the road, the bottom twelve feet of the building was decorated in shiny brown wall tiles that surrounded frosted ground-floor windows. His father had explained to him that originally it had been a pub called the Portobello that had closed down during the war. The building itself was three storeys high and stood on a corner. Its ground-floor entrance was off the main road on Alderson Street which was a cul-de-sac that ended with a six-foot brick wall topped with spiked railings. From the window of their top-floor flat, the boy could see a canal on the other side of the wall. His parents had warned him that he would face physical violence should he ever go near the canal.

Alderson Street had a terrace of five small houses. This terrace of single-storey houses lay between the tall building where the boy lived on the corner, and the canal wall. Everyone who lived on the street worked in Askey's factory with Conor's parents, and they were always very friendly to the little boy. When the opportunity arose, he would visit them one by one. His mother had heard about these visits, and warned him of a chastising if she found him doing this again. He made a conscious decision to ignore this threat. The way that he justified this to himself was that her warning was about her finding out, not of him actually doing it.

In particular he liked the families in the two houses at the end nearest the canal. The first of these was a Polish family, the Tomasevskis, and the end house was home to the Batemans who were from Trinidad. Anytime he called in to his neighbours, he dined on Polish sausage with tea at the Tomasevskis, and wonderful fried potatoes in the Batemans. There were no other children on the street, so he was spoilt whichever house he went into. Mrs Batemen used to tell the boy stories of herself as a young girl in Port Elizabeth, and Mr Tomasevski told him all about Gdansk, which was his home town in Poland.

Peter Tomasevski was built like a professional wrestler and kept homing pigeons that Conor helped him with. Although a giant of a man, Mr Tomasevski was very gentle with the birds. There was one bird in particular that was Conor's favourite, a beautiful young white bird with small brown flecks on his wings. In recognition of the boy's affinity to the bird, the Polish man let him name it, and Conor called it "Christopher". Mr Tomasevski had a large dark-grey motorcycle and sidecar, with an engine that made a deep throbbing sound. The man had explained to the boy that he trained the birds by taking them miles away from their loft, at the back of his house, and then releasing them. Each trip he would take the birds further and further away, but they always came back to their loft, and were waiting for him when he got back. The boy was enthralled with this and asked how the birds found their way back home. The Polish man smiled at the boy and simply said, "It is in their spirit."

Conor watched from the window of the flat for Mr Tomasevski on Saturday mornings. At eight o'clock each Saturday, the man carefully placed the pigeons into a small cage, and put them into the seat of the sidecar. The engine was kicked into life, and the man with his birds headed down the road for the ritual of release. The Bateman and Tomasevski families had very different stories to tell, one of beautiful sunshine with happy people and the other of a dull grey country with hardship and war.

*

The route to school was very familiar to the boy, and this morning the boy and his mother walked down the road past the high red brick walls and iron gates of Askey's factory. They continued the hundred yards to the junction of Ladbroke Grove, and then turned left across the railway bridge. The bridge was made of iron and painted a deep red colour. It was spattered with bulging rivets, and at either side of the road was a pedestrian pathway that was surrounded by metal plates and overhead arches with lanterns fitted on top. He could not see the road traffic on the bridge or the trains underneath, but he could hear the cars passing, and the squeal of the train's wheels as they cornered on the steel rails below him.

Up the road from the entrance to St Charles Square was a small sweet shop that Conor visited often.

The boy turned to his mother and asked, "Can I get a drink before school?"

"Alright but hurry up – you don't want to be late."

He went inside and up to the counter, which was at his eye level. The shopkeeper was familiar to the boy. Mr Sadhu was a tall Indian gentleman with a large turban and a beard that he kept in a white net around his chin.

"Can I have a raspberry drink, please?"

"Small or large?"

"Small, please."

The man reached for the red-coloured bottle and placed it on the green dimpled rubber matt on the counter. He then took a small tumbler and filled it to the brim.

"Halfpenny, please."

The boy handed him a new copper penny from his pocket. The till rang up ½ d and his change was placed beside the glass. He put the change into his pocket and drank down the fizzy drink in one long gulp.

"Thank you," said the boy and left the shop.

"You are very welcome," said the shopkeeper and he smiled as he watched the boy leave.

They walked down St Charles Square, with its rows of neat yellow-brick houses and white-railed fences, towards the school gate. Across the big iron gate was the St Charles crest, and the words *Semper Fidelis*, which he was told was Latin for 'always faithful'. His mother turned him around so that he faced her, and she tut-tutted as she took out her handkerchief. She licked the handkerchief and wiped the corners of his mouth. The boy hated this and it seemed to happen every morning.

His mother said, "I will meet you outside Miss McNamara's office at two o'clock – make sure and drink your milk and eat all of your dinner," and with that she turned and walked away.

Conor entered a playground that was teaming with grey uniformed youngsters of different sizes 'running' laughing and generally making huge amounts of noise. He looked through the window into the teachers' staffroom and saw Miss McNamara standing, talking with the other teachers. He wondered what she wanted to see them for today, but he shrugged his shoulders and walked towards his classroom.

Chapter 2

onor was sitting on a chair in the corridor outside Miss McNamara's office at ten minutes to two. There were a dozen or so chairs lined up along the corridor, and he sat on the end chair, closest to the principal's office. He was swinging his feet backwards and forwards under the chair. His grey knee-length socks were gathered in a bunch around his ankles and his coat and cap were on the chair beside him. The floor was a deep-wine-coloured linoleum, marbled with flecks of other colours, and it smelled strongly of lavender floor polish. The surface of the linoleum shone brightly from endless hours of buffing from the big polishing machine that he had seen the cleaning staff use.

At the end of the corridor and sitting in an alcove was a statue of the Sacred Heart. The figure had its hands raised about chest high, like it was gesturing with its hands for the viewer to stop and come no closer. From the thirty feet or so that he was away, the boy could see the red blood marks on each of the palms. On the head of the figure was a crown of thorns and there were lines of blood running down the forehead and cheeks, matting the long curly brown hair. The figure held its head slightly to one side and had large mournful eyes in a gaunt and drawn face. A beard covered the chin, and the figure had on wine-and white-coloured robes. The feet were barefoot with the same blood marks as on the hands, and the figure stood on top of a small, square, stone plinth. Above the statue's head was a golden halo that seemed to float above and behind it. The boy was tempted to walk up and look behind to see how the halo was held in place, but he resisted the temptation.

Directly in front of the statue, there were three rows of small, red, glass bowls. Some of these had candles inside and they lit up the end of the corridor with a flickering red light that danced on the walls. The candles competed with the floor polish to give the corridor the smell of a church. A box with a brass plate stood in front of the row of candles with a small slot on the top. Engraved on the plate were the words, "Donations for St Charles Church Fund".

The boy heard the door open at the other end of the corridor, and saw his mother come in. She was wearing the outfit she normally wore going out at the weekends, which consisted of a short-brown-suede coat over a cream jumper and a deep red tartan skirt. On her head she had a matching small suede hat, and on her feet she wore tan high-heeled shoes. She made her way towards him trying to walk on tiptoe, but she still made a tapping sound against the floor with every step as she moved along the corridor. She took the boy's hat and coat off the chair, put them on her lap and sat down beside him. She was wearing makeup, the highlight of which was a splash of bright red lipstick.

She leaned across towards him and said out of the side of her mouth, "For God's sake pull up your socks, or you will make a holy show of us." The boy pulled up both socks and then continued swinging his legs to and fro under the chair. His mother leaned across again and whispered, "Do you know what this is about?" Before he had a chance to answer, she turned to look at him directly and said, "You are not in any trouble are you, because I will kill you if you are."

The boy looked at her and said, "I don't think so."

She kept looking at him and nodded her head up and down in rhythm to her words as she said through pursed lips, "Well if it's a thing that you have been up to ..." but before she had a chance to finish, Miss McNamara popped her head out of the door. Without even breaking sentence, the boy's mother said, "Miss McNamara, delighted to see you again." The boy noticed that not only the tone was different, but the accent had changed as well.

"Delighted to see you too, Mrs O'Loughlin. Please come this way," and she escorted the boy and his mother into her office.

Miss McNamara was a short, plump lady, who always seemed to be dressed in the same way. She wore her hair in a style that looked like the picture of the queen on a postage stamp, and she had on a navy blue, tweed suit with a white, frilly blouse and a string of large pearls tight against her throat. Her shoes were black and chunky and squeaked as she walked on the linoleum.

Conor and his mother were directed to sit on the two chairs in front of the headmistress's desk and they took their seats. The mother had the boy's coat and hat neatly folded across her lap. The desktop had a deep green leather inlay with some books and pens all neatly placed around a large ink blotter. Around the walls were silver trophies and cups along with pictures of various figures shaking hands with the headmistress. In each picture, St Charles School was in the background. The boy was sitting with his hands under his thighs, swinging his legs, and looking around the office. All around him he could get the smell of camphor from mothballs, sweet perfume and the same lavender polish as the corridor. It was a bright sunny day and the sunlight shone in through the venetian blinds on the window behind the teacher's back.

Miss McNamara looked directly at the boy's mother and clasping her hands, with her fingers entwined, she spoke: "Thank you so much for coming at such short notice, Mrs O'Loughlin, and sorry about all the mystery."

His mother replied, "Not at all. I just hope that Conor has been behaving himself. We are very happy with him here at St Charles."

The headmistress seemed to be taken aback and leaned forward with her hands still clasped. She placed both her elbows on the desk. "Been behaving himself," she repeated. "Oh sorry, Mrs O'Loughlin, but it is in fact the opposite."

"How do you mean, Miss McNamara?" asked the boy's mother.

"I called you in because it is my view and the view of the teaching staff, that Conor is an intellectually gifted child or an IGC as we say in the trade."

The mother looked a little confused, "What does that mean?"

"We grade our pupils relative to how old they are, and we watch closely if they are intellectually ahead or behind of where they should be for their age. We find some are normal, some behind and some are ahead."

"So Conor is ahead of his age."

"Yes, we would define Conor as being in the IGC category."

"How far ahead is he?" She asked this as she looked at the boy who was swinging his legs under the chair and looking around the room.

"In this particular case, we have difficulty in measuring it. I honestly don't think there is a class in the school that would challenge him. Here, please let me give you an example." She picked up a book from the desk and leafed through the pages.

When she had found the place that she wanted, she turned the book around with her finger pointing to a paragraph and said, "Conor, will you read from here for me please?"

The boy took the book and in a clear and precise voice spoke, "Let me see. Alas, poor Yorick! I knew him, Horatio, a fellow of infinite jest, of most excellent fancy. He hath borne me on his back a thousand times, and now, how abhorred in my imagination it is! My gorge rises at it. Here hung those lips that I have kissed I know not how oft."

The teacher stopped him with a "Thank you", and took the book from him and placed it on the desk.

"Conor, what do you think this passage is about?"

The boy thought for a while and asked, "Who is speaking, Miss?"

"It is Hamlet, the Prince of Denmark," she replied.

The boy seemed to be deep in thought for a while, and looked to one side of the teacher as he spoke. "Hamlet is speaking to Horatio, about an old friend of his – Yorick. Yorick was a part of Hamlet's life and he described his old friend as funny and playful. He says that Yorick had often carried him on his back, which could mean that Yorick was Hamlet's friend when he was a child."

Again the boy paused, "I think Hamlet is looking at an image of his old friend, but it is the image of a changed Yorick, because Hamlet is both sad and sickened by the sight."

The boy stopped and refocused his look back to the teacher.

"Thank you, Conor." The teacher smiled at the boy, and turned to look at the boy's mother, "Do you see what I mean, Mrs O'Loughlin?"

His mother was looking at the boy in disbelief.

"Mrs O'Loughlin, an eight-year-old should not be able to read a passage like that from Shakespeare, let alone be able to interpret it."

The mother was silent for a little while and then asked, "Is this a good thing or a bad thing?"

The teacher smiled at her and said, "That is a very good question. It is without doubt a gift and must be nurtured. I called you in because I wanted you to understand this. It is important that he gets plenty of books to read and keeps himself occupied. Children like Conor get bored very easily unless they are intellectually challenged. I will make sure that he gets appropriate books from the school here that he can take home to read."

The boy's mother looked at the teacher and asked, "Are you going to move him up a class?"

"I discussed this with his teachers, and we decided against it. It would be unfair on the boy to put him with students who are more mature physically, and when it becomes evident that he is much brighter than they are, it might make it difficult on him."

"You mean bullying?"

"Unfortunately, yes, we will just let him develop with children of his own age."

The teacher looked at the boy and smiling turned back to the mother and said, "Do you know what he does during break time?"

The boy's mother shook her head and said, "No."

"He heads off with Tom the caretaker and works with him around the school. Tom is a wonderful man. He is very patient and would have made a great teacher himself. He has told me that this chap fires thousands of questions at him. They are the best of pals."

The teacher looked down at her desk and said with a hint of a smile, "Only once before have I come across a pupil of his age with his intellect, a little girl called Margaret."

"How did she do?"

"I don't know. It was during the war – she disappeared and I never saw her again."

The teacher smiled warmly and said as she pointed to the boy, "Ones like these are very much like finding a large pearl in an oyster."

She straightened up and said, "I will be meeting you at parent – teacher reviews, but please make sure that he is kept very busy reading and writing. We want to keep him challenged."

The headmistress rose, reached across the desk and shook the woman's hand.

"Thank you very much, Miss McNamara."

"Please call me Joan."

"Then please call me May," the boy's mother replied.

The mother and son got up, and the boy reached across the desk to shake hands with the teacher and said, "Thank you, Miss."

The headmistress gave a little laugh as she shook the boy's hand.

The boy and his mother walked out of the office and closed the door behind them. As they did, one of the boy's socks fell down around his ankle. He bent down to pull it up and said, "Sorry."

His mother looked at him and said in a quiet voice, "It's all right." She stopped, held his coat open for him and he put it on. She then gently placed his cap on his head, and the two walked along the corridor and out the door into the schoolyard.

Chapter 3

As the summer approached in 1961, life in London continued as normal for the little boy, but he now had the added responsibility of getting himself to and from school. This meant he was entrusted with the keys to the flat, and this arrangement suited him admirably. His mother had taken to working full-time, and this provided the boy with the additional bonus of three hours in the afternoon where he could explore the building he lived in unsupervised and uninterrupted. His father worked from early in the morning to late in the evening, so the only time he saw him was at the weekends when they went into London shopping or visited his father's sister in Hammersmith. Conor loved his Aunt Claire and looked forward to these visits with great anticipation. It was a very short journey by tube from Ladbroke Grove to where his aunt lived in Biscay Road.

Claire was a very tall, elegant lady with long-red wavy hair that she kept loosely tied up. She wore bright, vibrant coloured clothes and lived with her English husband, Keith, and their two daughters, Emily and Kate, in a small flat. She had moved to London from Ireland a few years before Conor's father when she was just sixteen. Claire's husband was a very quiet man with a north of England accent. He always wore a leather jacket, and he had two large scars on his forehead as the result of a motorcycle accident. There was an electric train set that was permanently set up in their sitting room, and the boy used to love to see the man operate it. Keith said very little and smiled to himself a lot, but Conor liked him, although the boy's parents appeared to be very awkward when Keith was around.

His cousins were very bright and bubbly girls. Conor enjoyed Kate as she was about his own age, with Emily a little older and more aloof. Kate had her mother's wavy red hair, while Emily was dark like her father. To the boy, the flat on Biscay Road was spectacular. It was filled with a large record collection and books were stuffed on shelves everywhere. His aunt worked as a teacher, and always found time to talk with the boy. These conversations were about everything and anything but always as equals, which he enjoyed enormously. She asked his opinions on things like travelling the tube and school, and she offered her advice on music and reading but never in a dictatorial way. She brewed her own coffee, and showed him the process of grinding the beans and how to use the percolator. He sat on the stool in the kitchen and waited for the water to spurt out of the tube of the percolator, hit the glass top and flow down through the ground coffee and back into the body of the pot. The stool in the kitchen was his favourite spot, and he loved to sit and watch his aunt as she made sandwiches for them when they visited. She showed him how to make baked apples with cinnamon and fruit. The boy was part of the preparation process where his aunt would scoop out the centre of each apple, and he would stuff them with the fruit mixture that they had prepared.

Claire read him selected poems and passages from her vast collection of books and would ask his opinion. She would always give him a book to take away and read, and she played records for him whenever they visited. He soon had his own favourite songs that she would play for him. The smell of coffee brewing and the sound of Pete Seeger singing "Little Boxes" were the memories of Claire that the boy always kept with him. As long as he could remember they visited Claire every other week, but it had been months now since they had gone to Biscay Road. He recalled that there had been a row between the brother and sister the last time they had visited, and on this occasion Conor's mother had also got involved. There was always an uneasy tension between Pat and Claire, but it had turned very nasty on that particular occasion which upset the boy greatly. His father and mother stormed out of the flat on Biscay Road bringing the boy with them, and they had not returned since.

The little boy missed visiting his aunt very much, but he had some books she had given him that he would read diligently every day. There was something very special about her, and apart from the last visit, every time he visited Biscay Road was magical for him. It puzzled him why brother and sister were so different.

The boy's parents were very focused on their work, and their limited social life consisted of shopping in London or an occasional visit to the local pub at the weekends. Claire, however, used to travel around London on the bicycle that she kept in the hallway of the flat. She had promised him that when he was old enough she would take him on a cycling trip around London. His aunt rarely, if ever, spoke of Ireland, but she did speak of a longing that she had to live in a small cottage in the north of Scotland. Quite often she would travel up there on the train and visit friends. On these trips she always took her bicycle, which the men from British Rail would put in the guards van of the train for her. She told the boy that on one occasion she was at Victoria Station and had her bicycle with her ready to travel.

The man taking her ticket on the platform said to her, "Sorry madam, you can't bring your bicycle onto the train."

The boy asked wide-eyed, "What did you do?"

She replied, "I just said, 'Don't be silly,' and I continued walking."

"Were you able to get your bike on the train? Did he try to stop you?" he asked.

"Of course I got my bike on the train." She nudged the boy with her elbow and grinned. "What a silly little man he was."

He kept those happy memories of his aunt with him always.

With his parents at work, Conor would arrive in from school at about two o'clock and go upstairs and turn on the big radio in the kitchen. The radio took a little while to warm up, but soon the sombre voice of the BBC News would fill the room. The news terrified him at times, with talk of nuclear war between Russia and America, and special programmes with instructions of what to do in the event of a nuclear attack. The news was then followed by the shipping forecast, "Tyne, Dogger, Fisher, German Bight – falling slowly". Conor found the radio to be both terrifying and intensely boring at the same time. There was a programme in the afternoon that was called *Listen with Mother*, and the little boy found this to be more boring than the shipping forecast. His main focus on a daily basis was to explore the empty floors of the building underneath the flat.

On one particular afternoon, he found his way downstairs to the ground floor, and was searching around in the hallway at the bottom of the stairs. He had never managed to get into the ground floor, as there did not seem to be a doorway in. On this day, however, he noticed that at the side of the stairs there was a narrow gap between the banister and the wall. He slipped between them and found himself under the stairwell. It was lit by a small frosted glass window and there was dust everywhere. Facing him he could make out a door that was made of dark timber on the bottom and frosted glass on top. It was slightly ajar and he put his fingers into the gap and pulled it towards him. With a loud creak it opened and standing about four feet in front of him was a wooden panel with the same frosted glass across the top. Engraved on the glass in the shape of an arc was the word "Portobello". He made his way along and around the panel, and turned to find himself looking into the remains of what used to be a pub.

The boy was ecstatic with the discovery, and he made his way gingerly across the creaky timber floor. The place was strewn with broken chairs and tables, but to his right the high counter was intact. There was dust and debris everywhere, but the optics for the spirits were still on the wall and the long brass and timber beer pump handles were on the high counter. It was like being in heaven for the little boy. He found a chair that was still intact and used it to climb up and onto the bar where he stood up to look around. From this vantage point he could survey the entire place. He could see a piano in the corner and empty beer crates were all around.

Along the top of the side wall were windows that were fitted with frosted glass. These windows let enough light in to give the place a kind of ghostly feel, but it was still bright enough for him to see all around the place. There was the smell of musty stale beer everywhere. He kicked the pieces of broken furniture off the counter onto the floor. He went over to the long beer tap handles and pushed one of them with his foot. It was stiff but it moved in an arc towards the bar and made a sucking sound. He pulled it towards him and it made a slightly different sound. It came to rest in an upright position. There were four pump handles and the boy tried each one in turn with the same result. Behind the bar were some glass shelves and a long mirror that stretched the length of the counter. The mirror was very dusty, but perfectly intact. In the centre of the mirror he could make out the same lettering "Portobello" that was on the frosted glass at the entrance. He could just about see his own reflection in the mirror and he was grinning from ear to ear.

He stood and turned around a number of times on the bar counter so that he could take it all in. As he looked around, he knew with great certainty that this was going to be his place. He also knew that he needed to keep the Portobello a secret from everyone. He could not suppress his feelings. They were a mixture of adventure and excitement but a great sense of belonging too. After a long time of just looking around him at this new and magical place, he climbed down off the bar counter onto the chair. He then made his way across the debris on the floor and back outside to under the stairs. Slipping through the space between the banister and the wall, he went upstairs to wait for his mother.

Chapter 4

Each weekday afternoon from two o'clock to half past four, the boy cleaned and put the Portobello into order. It was his nature to tidy and organise, and the work was great fun for him. He had found a back door that led into a walled-off yard. To one side of the yard was a roofed section that was piled with more broken furniture, mirrors and stacks of sodden beer mats with the words "Watney's Best Bitter" and "A Fistful of Flavour" printed on them. Bits of beer pumps and tubes were strewn everywhere, and a metal cabinet stood against the wall. The first task he undertook was to clear space in the yard for the broken furniture and beer crates, and this he did with much enthusiasm.

After some effort he put the yard into reasonable shape, and he found himself standing in front of the metal cabinet. He tried the handle which opened quite easily, and he was hit immediately with a very strong musty smell. On the shelves of the cabinet were rows of green masks that had goggles and tubes. He recognised these as gas masks from pictures of the war he had seen at school. The masks frightened him, and he turned away from the cabinet and got sick. He closed the cabinet, and vowed never to open it again. His mood lifted when he started moving the broken furniture from the bar into the yard and he could begin to see the Portobello taking shape.

He soon had a routine going for fixing up the place. As soon as he arrived in from school he would start clearing and cleaning. Diligently he would check his watch and leave at half past four to wash up before his mother got in at five o'clock. He learned this lesson the hard way, when his mother arrived home one day to see him black from head to toe, and delivered him a swift blow to the ear. After this, he found some old bar aprons and was very careful to wear one of these when working. He also made sure to wash himself before she arrived. The apron was much too big for him, but he wrapped it tightly around him and tied it at the front. The bar clean-up went on for two weeks, until eventually he had the pub – still looking a little grey and dusty – but much closer to how it looked when it was last open. He had even managed, courtesy of some borrowed cloths and polish from upstairs, to clean and shine the counter. He rubbed down the brass on the beer pumps and foot rail until they shone.

When he had finished he sat up onto the bar counter and surveyed the scene. The floor was swept and there were two tables still intact with three chairs apiece. The piano was not in great shape in the corner. You could see missing keys and its strings and hammers were exposed, but it was polished as best as he could manage. As he looked across the floor from the bar, the entire wall facing him was stacked to the ceiling with empty beer crates. He thought his next job would be to move these out into the yard. He considered how he was going to do this, as he had no ladder to get up to the top and start taking them down. Checking his watch he saw it was almost half past four and decided it was a job for tomorrow. He took off his apron and went upstairs to wash up.

As he lay awake that night he was thinking about the stack of beer crates. He thought: if I stand on a chair and pull on the middle crate, because they are locked together, they should all fall down – just like a tree falling when it is cut. He thought further: but I will have to put the chair to one side, or I will be pulling the lot down on me. He figured an injury would be very hard to explain away. He considered the possibility that the crates could crash onto the bar counter and damage it, or they might even break the mirror behind the bar. The boy eventually drifted off to sleep without resolving the problem.

That next afternoon Conor sat on the bar and looked at the beer crate mountain in front of him. He was trying to understand how far into the room the crates would end up when they fell to the floor. He went out into the yard, picked up a beer crate, brought it in and placed it in the middle of the floor. Standing back he looked at it with his hands on his hips. He decided that if the crates were to fall they would fall on their side, so he turned the crate on its side and stood back again. He pushed it forward until it touched the first stack of crates and sat back on the bar. It was then it came to him. If he brought in the same number of crates that were stacked up and lay them out on the floor, this would show him where the stack of crates would end up. He counted fifteen crates high, brought in that number and stacked them flat on their side along the floor. He saw that they did not even go half way across the floor, and so he swiftly moved everything off the floor and into the yard, except for the one chair that was going to be his ladder.

He placed the chair to one side of the first stack, climbed onto it, grabbed a crate and tried to pull it forward. It rocked a little but did not budge. He got down and with hands on hips looked at this next problem. He thought that if he could reach higher it would be easier to pull down the stack, but what would he use? He remembered there was a wooden pole with a brass hook on its end out in the yard and he fetched it in. Standing on the chair he stretched out the pole and hooked it into the highest crate he could reach, and gave an almighty tug. The crates seemed to fall very slowly and at the same time as they were falling, the boy was rocking dramatically backward and forward on the chair desperately trying to stay upright. Amid this scene of toppling crates, and the boy flailing his arms trying to stop from falling off the chair, the crates crashed to the floor with a loud bang and a plume of dust. A wide grin spread across his face and he jumped down to remove the crates out into the yard.

He repeated this for the next two stacks, and found that behind the crates was a long heavy curtain that seemed to reach from ceiling to floor. It was a deep red colour with a gold border on the bottom and a large box pelmet at the top. Glancing at his watch he saw it was nearly half past four so he abandoned the work for the day. He removed his apron and ran upstairs for the wash-up ritual.

The next afternoon he continued pulling down the crates and removing them into the yard. He took care to make sure he kept the outside tidy, so he stacked the crates as high as he could around the walls of the yard. When he had all the crates removed, he sat on the bar and looked across at the big red curtain. It took up over half the wall and had deep folds that reached from under the pelmet to where it swept the ground. He thought that every curtain he had ever seen was divided in two. Jumping off the bar he ran his hands along the curtain from left to right. He could feel no separation, so he thought further and then ran his hands along from right to left. About half way across, his hands disappeared behind the left curtain; he had found the overlap. The curtains were quite heavy and when he tried to pull them apart he was not able. They seemed to be weighted somehow on the bottom, so he got back and sat on the bar again to figure out how he was going to open the curtains and see what lay behind.

As he pondered, he remembered his Aunt Claire's curtains in Biscay Road. He studied her very closely in everything she did, and he remembered that when she would close the curtains in the front window, she reached behind them and pulled down on a cord and they closed with a swoosh. He remembered this, because once he went behind them to investigate and found the cord. When he emerged from behind the closed curtain there was much laughter as his aunt and cousins had been following the moving lump in the curtain with some amusement.

Getting down off the bar again, he went to the left and felt behind the curtain for a cord and could find none. He then went to the right and ran his hand all around and even went behind the curtain. As he reached up, his hand touched something more like a rope than a cord. It was quite high so he brought in his chair behind the curtain, stood on it and pulled down on the rope. The curtains fluttered a little but did not open. He ran his hands along the rope and found that it was a loop. He pulled down on the rope but again all he got was a little flutter. Without really thinking why, he tried from the other side of the loop and the rope moved freely. The curtains parted slowly, and he fell off the chair in a heap.

After a few attempts he realised that if you pull on the loop from one side the curtains opened, and from the other side they closed. When this was figured out, he kept pulling on the rope to open the curtains until they could move no further. He emerged with his chair and looked at what was behind the curtain. His mouth fell open when he saw it was in fact a stage. He sat back on his spot on the bar and what he saw all across the back of the stage was a painting of a blue sky and a mountain. In front of this on the stage, was the back and side walls of a log cabin complete with a window and a door. The window had red-and-white checked curtains, and the door was a half door similar to some he had seen before on the summer trips to Ireland. There were blue patterned plates standing upright on an old dresser against the log wall, and, further out onto the stage, was a small round table with two chairs. There was a bottle in a small basket and it was all covered in white candle grease. On the table was a cloth of the same checked material as the curtains.

Bounding off the bar with his eyes blazing, he jumped onto the stage via the chair, and ran around at full tilt. He sat at the table and looked at the bar which looked completely different from here. He ran around the stage again, stopped in the middle, turned to face the bar and sang a verse of "Sean South of Garryowen" at the top of his voice.

T'was on a dreary New Year's Day as the shades of light fell down,
A lorry load of volunteers approached the border town,
There were men from Dublin and from Cork, Fermanagh and Tyrone,
And the foremost of that gallant band was South from Garryowen.

Realising the time, he jumped off the stage, looked back at his new discovery and dashed upstairs just in time for a wash up before the five o'clock deadline.

That night he slept very peacefully because although he was very excited, he was also exhausted. Twice he was called for school the next morning, and eventually he got up and crept to school. At school, however, and as it got closer to two o'clock, he grew very excited at the prospect of revisiting the Portobello.

Chapter 5

The boy spent a lot of time brushing and cleaning down the stage. An empty whiskey bottle from behind the bar and one of the very few remaining unbroken glasses were placed on the table. When the sun shone, it streamed light onto the stage through the frosted windows. He read books and poems aloud, sang songs and danced about. The wooden boards seemed to move with him so that he could spring around and jump very high. Sometimes he would just sit at the table and look at the bar across from him, and other times he would sit on the bar and look at the stage. His afternoons were filled with joy, and every day was an adventure for him.

One afternoon when he was dancing around on the stage, he spotted that there was a cut-out on the side of the stage floor close to the outside wall. He followed the split in the boards and thought that perhaps the cut-out could be a door. He found a metal flap that was level with the floor boards. He could see a little notch that he stuck his finger into and lifted it up. Under this was a brass ring that was home to a couple of huge spiders that scuttled away when they were exposed to the light. He pulled up the ring out of its pocket so he could grab it with his hands. Grabbing the ring with both hands he pulled, but it did not budge. It was then he realised he was standing on the door and was trying to lift himself. He laughed out loud, stood aside and tried the brass ring again. The door lifted very easily with a creaking sound that seemed to come from two long springs at either side of the door. When he had it lifted about half way, it opened up fully by itself and stayed upright. He could not figure out how this worked, but he thought it had something to do with the springs that functioned in the same way as the boot of his father's Ford Prefect.

Underneath the door was a steep set of ten or so concrete steps. It was quite dark, but undeterred he ventured down the steps into the darkness. When he reached the bottom of the steps, directly in front of him was what appeared to be a wall. The wall felt very warm and smooth to the touch. It was dark, so he was feeling as much as seeing. His hand came to rest on a large key sticking out of what he could now see was not a wall, but a door. He grabbed the key and tried to push and pull at the door but nothing was moving. He tried to turn the key and it moved a little but no further. Twisting it back again, it came out from the keyhole. After a few attempts the key was reinserted, and he tried to twist it again, but it only moved back to its original position. Taking out the key, he put it in his trouser pocket and resolved to enlist the help of Tom, the school caretaker, in finding a solution. Tom was the boy's friend, and a genius of all things mechanical. He thought to himself, if there is a way to get the door open Tom will know. After closing down the door on the stage, he put the flap into place and went upstairs. As he scrubbed himself the boy was determined that the door would be opened, and he could not wait to see what was on the other side.

As he lay in bed waiting for the call to get up for school,

a thought came to him: what if the door simply opens out onto Kensal Road? On his way to school the next morning, he checked but could see no sign of a door outside, so he assumed if it opened at all, it opened into a passageway or even under the road. He continued on to school and immediately sought out Tom the caretaker.

Tom was standing outside his tool shed drinking a mug of tea, and the boy went over to him. The caretaker was a big burly man with curly, grey-red hair and giant sideburns. He always seemed to be talking to himself, but he was very popular with the pupils and teachers alike. In particular Conor and Tom had always got along very well, and they had some great conversations about how things worked. The man was always willing to explain things in detail to the boy and was very kind and patient. That was why the boy often sought him out during break times and helped him with his various jobs around the school.

As the boy went over to him he said, "Excuse me, Tom, can I ask you a question?"

"So long as it's not too complicated, young Conor."

The boy smiled, "I have a door at home, and the key won't turn and unlock it."

Tom thought for a little while and closing one eye looked at the boy and said, "Are you sure it is the right key?"

The boy had not considered this, and said, "I think it is. It was left in the door and it turns a little in the lock." He reached into his pocket and handed the key to the man.

"It is a very old key, and there is a lot of rust on it," and he looked at the boy again with one eye closed and said, "You are not up to any mischief are you?"

The boy simply said, "I just want to see what is on the other side."

Tom looked at him and smiled, "I suppose that is a good enough reason to open any door." He handed the key back to the boy as he set down his mug of tea on the window ledge. He went inside the shed and came back out with a lock and key in his hand.

Tom turned the key in the lock and the square locking bolt popped out, turned it back again and it popped back. "Is there a handle on the door?"

"No, just the key."

"OK, then all you have is this part", and he circled around the key and square locking bolt with his finger. He reached into his overalls, took out a screwdriver and opened up the lock. With his large hands he showed how the key moved the matching cams to push the locking bolt forwards and pull it backwards. "The probable reason why your key won't turn is because the mechanism is rusted and it is stuck together."

"How do I open it, then?"

"You need to oil it so that the parts move freely."

"But I can't get in at it like that," and he pointed to the lock in the caretaker's hands.

"How do you think you might do it then?" Tom asked.

The boy thought for a little while and said, "If I had a little oilcan with a narrow little tube, somehow I could squirt the oil in through the keyhole."

"Good thinking. Let me see what I have."

Tom went into the shed and emerged with a miniature copper oilcan. It was round and flat and fitted into the palm of the man's hand. There was a knurled brass cap at the top, which was where the can was filled with oil, and a very thin brass tube which was bent at the end.

"Watch this," said Tom, and he placed the tube of the can into the keyhole and turned it upwards at the cams. He placed his fingers either side of the flat body and pressed. The can moved inward and snapped out again when he released it. He did this rapidly with the can between his fingers, and the boy could see oil spurt out of the little pipe and into the lock. The boy grinned from ear to ear, and Tom smiled at him. "I will fill this little chap with oil. There are lots of different types of oil you know, but I think this job needs penetrating oil. The secret with penetrating oil is that it is not thick and will get into small spaces. The important thing is to get it into the right place and let it soak into the lock." He paused and said, "You will need to get the oil in there and let it soak – overnight would be best."

The caretaker paused for a while and said, "OK, so you say there is no handle. I do not know how the door opens, so you will have to pull it open or pull it closed with the key. Here, let me show you." He took the lock in one hand, put in the key, turning it only a little and pulled the lock with the key. "There is one last thing that you will need, and that is a little help in turning the key for the first time." Tom produced a little steel bar out of his pocket. "Show me the key again," he said. The boy handed him the key and the man said, "When you are trying to open the lock for the first time it will be stiff, so you will need a little help from this." He took the key and placed the bar through the key's ring and with his other hand showed the boy how to grab the end of the bar for leverage. "Just be very careful not to put too much pressure on, or the key might break. I think you are all set then." He went into the shed and brought out a little canvas bag. Into this he placed the little can, which now had a plastic cap to stop the oil from spilling out of the spout, along with the bar in a neatly folded cloth. He handed the bag and the key to the boy, and said, "Good luck, then, young Conor, and remember to be gentle, and when you do get the key to unlock the door, lock and unlock it a number of times until it is easy to turn with the key alone."

"Thank you, Tom, I will bring these back to you."

"No, it is OK, you keep them and start your own tool collection."

The boy smiled and said, "I will look after them," and with that he ran off across the playground just as the bell for class was sounding. The caretaker watched him run off and picking up his cup of tea smiled and said to himself, "God only knows what he is up to."

As soon as Conor got home, he went into the pub and set down the bag Tom had given him onto the table of the stage. He opened up the door on the stage but it was quite dark down there. It was then that he remembered the torch that they kept in the kitchen drawer of the flat. He ran upstairs to retrieve it and brought it back downstairs. Armed with the torch and his bag of tools, he climbed down the steps and with the torch he was able to inspect the door more closely. Taking the little can, he removed the plastic cap and placed it on the cloth. Then with the torch in one hand and the can in the other, he put the spout of the can into the keyhole, tilted it upwards and started pressing the can in the way Tom had shown him. He kept pressing for what seemed a long time, as he wanted to make sure he was getting oil in there. It was not until he saw oil running out of the keyhole and down the door did he stop. He squirted oil on the key and placed it into the keyhole. He put the little plastic cap back onto the spout of the can, and placed it along with the cloth and bar back into the bag. He brought them back up onto the stage, switched off the torch and left them all on the table. Jumping off the stage he sat up onto the bar and felt a real excitement at the prospect of finding out what lay on the other side of the door.

Chapter 6

It was ten minutes past two, and it had been a full day since he had oiled the lock. He stood in front of the door with the torch in one hand and the steel bar in the other. He put the bar through the key and pushed down on it. It creaked and moved slightly. He pushed the bar in the other direction and the key moved backward. Heeding Tom's advice, he pushed on the bar lightly and every time he did, the key moved a little further and was always accompanied by a creak. He kept at this for ten minutes until finally the key turned. The door opened slightly in towards him, and sunlight flooded the dark space under the stage. He pushed the door closed and worked the key with the bar so that the door locked again. He did this over and over again until he could easily open and close the door with just the key.

Climbing back onto the stage, he sat for a little and said to himself, "Now is the time." So he decided to put on his school cap and venture forth. He was just making his way down towards the door when he realised he had his apron on. Laughing at this, he took off the apron, placed it on the chair, straightened his cap and started down the steps. He faced the door and put in the key, opened the door and using the key, pulled it towards him.

Outside was bright sunshine and it felt very hot and humid. He was facing a steep set of concrete steps that were painted dark blue. He took out the key from inside the door and placed it into the lock, pulled the door closed and locked it from outside. Pocketing the key he crept up the steps one by one until he could peak over to see what lay beyond. He was looking out onto a street, but this was like no street he had ever seen before, and it certainly was not Kensal Road. He was near a corner and could see a set of yellow traffic lights with a green sign. Written on the green sign in bold white letters were the words "BLEECKER STREET". The concrete steps felt very hot and he stood up and climbed up onto the footpath.

At first he was disoriented and he wanted to turn around and go back inside, but he fought against this. He moved close to the wall of the building and stayed in the shade. The street was deserted but he could hear some noises of shouting in the distance. He looked all around him and he could see brightly coloured shops and doorways, but nothing that he recognised. He stood in the shade for a while just trying to take it all in and get his bearings. After a while, the shouting that he had heard from the end of the street seemed to be getting closer, and people came into view. They were running along the street with white boards and wooden poles, but nobody took any notice of the little boy in the grey school uniform.

He came out of the shade and looked back down the steps to make sure that the door was still there. It was painted black, with the number 248 painted on it in large white numbers. He stopped there for a while just trying to figure out where he was, but it baffled him. There were more loud voices coming from the end of the street, and he could hear the sound of galloping horses. In the distance, he could see two white horses with riders that were dressed all in blue. As they came closer, he saw that they wore shiny helmets that sparkled in the bright sunlight.

Around the corner from his right side, came a man with a white board under his arm and he ran past the boy without noticing him. One of the horsemen stopped in the middle of the road and turned his horse sideways to block the road, while the other galloped past. The second horseman then pulled up and jumped down off his horse. When the man with the board saw the horseman blocking the road, he turned and ran back towards where the boy was standing, but he ran straight towards the second horseman. The two met in the middle of the road not far from Conor, and it was then that the boy noticed that the man in blue had a long black stick in his hand. To the boy's horror, he took the stick and struck the man a sickening blow across the head. The board fell from the man's hands and he dropped to his knees. As he knelt on the ground, the figure in blue struck a flurry of blows across the man's head, driving him onto the ground. Each blow made a hollow sound that echoed all around the street. Conor could see dark blood oozing out of the man's mouth and ear onto the road. Eventually the horseman stopped, and put the black stick onto his belt. Turning around he noticed the little boy, and said, "Hey kid, get back home straight away, and tell your folks to stay indoors and away from the square." The little boy was terrified and just nodding ran back down the steps. With trembling hands he opened the door, slipped inside and after three attempts, which included dropping the key twice, he locked the door behind him. He closed down the door on the stage, ran out of the pub and raced up the stairs where he went straight into his room and lay sobbing on his bed.

Conor's mother came home from work to find the boy in bed trembling.

"What's wrong, Conor?" she asked.

The boy was bathed in sweat and kept muttering to himself about the square. The next few days were a blur to him, other than some fleeting images of being in a taxi on the way to hospital and doctors in white coats. He remembered being in St Mary's hospital in Paddington having x-rays and endless blood tests. All the time his mother was with him, and he could see by her face that she was very worried. The journey he had taken through the door was becoming hazy to him, but no matter how he tried to block it out, he had a vivid image of the man on the ground, bloody and beaten.

The next few days were spent at home from school, but the cause of his condition remained a mystery. He did not tell anyone about his experience, because he still wanted to keep the Portobello as his secret. For the first few days he had nightmares about what he had seen, but as the days went by he was able to put it to the back of his mind and his life seemed to be returning to normal. Despite tests from the hospital that showed things to be OK with the boy's health, his mother was not satisfied that things were all right with him, so she insisted on paying a visit to the family doctor.

The family doctor was Dr Hennegan, who was an old man with a very soft gentle voice. He had a head of unruly, steel-grey hair and always wore a matching silk handkerchief and tie. The handkerchief seemed to cascade out of his top pocket. Conor stood in front of his desk with his mother sitting on a chair beside him. The boy noticed that today the doctor wore a yellow bow tie with matching handkerchief and braces. The smell in the doctor's office was a mixture of boiled sweets and disinfectant. There was a white folding screen in the corner that was half open and behind it you could see a narrow bed, complete with a red rubber mattress. Alongside the narrow bed was a trolley with a number of metal instruments and syringes neatly laid out beside white, kidney-shaped bowls and a large, glass jar of cotton wool.

Conor's mother described the events of the past few days, and handed the doctor a large white envelope with some reports from the hospital in Paddington. The old man placed the glasses that were on a gold chain around his neck on the end of his nose as he studied the contents. His lips moved but he made no sound as he read, and eventually he put the bundle of papers down and turned to the little boy.

"Come here, Conor," the doctor said and he positioned the boy alongside him as he sat at his desk. He got the boy to take off his shirt and listened to his heart and lungs. He gently pulled down his bottom eyelids with his thumbs and looked into his eyes. With a flat stick he pressed down his tongue while getting the boy to say "Ahhh" at the same time. The old man sat back and told the boy to put his shirt back on.

He took the boy to the centre of the room and sat him down on a chair. The doctor took another chair and sat directly in front of him. Only then did he speak, "All right, Conor, tell me what have you been up to?"

"Nothing."

The doctor was looking at the boy over the top of his glasses and stayed this way for a while. "Is there anything wrong at school? Have the boys been picking on you? Is there anything worrying you?"

"No."

The old man watched very closely for his responses and stayed looking at him for a while. Eventually he turned to the mother, "I cannot see that there is anything physically wrong with him. Maybe he has had a shock of some kind, but at the moment there is no way that you are going to get anything out of him."

The doctor paused and said, "If something has happened he has locked it away, perhaps he will tell you in his own time. How is he doing at school, Mrs O'Loughlin?"

"Very well, Doctor. The teachers think he has great potential."

"Even so, I would get them to keep an eye out for bullying, just in case. I would not discount a virus of some sort either, so bring him back to me in a couple of weeks for a check-up."

After this episode, life returned to normal for the little boy, and he went back to school. Initially he could not enter the pub downstairs, but he missed it so much that eventually he ventured back. From then on, all of his afternoons were spent in the Portobello downstairs, but he never went near the door again. After a while he succeeded in blotting the incident out of his mind as if it had never happened.

Part 2

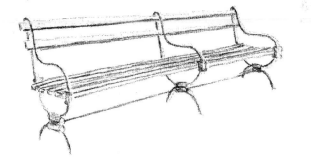

Chapter 7

It was approaching the summer of 1967 and Conor was now fourteen years old, top of the Third Form and a tall, slim teenager. His long, black hair curled around his face and neck, and the blue eyes still sparkled with energy and adventure. This Monday morning he was sitting on a tube train that rattled along between Paddington and Ladbroke Grove. He was dressed in his grey school shirt and slacks, complete with blue and gold striped tie. His school tie was permanently knotted, which meant that he just had to slip it over his head each morning. He found this to be very practical, but it meant that the tie hung loosely around his neck and the knot had become so small and tight that it had almost disappeared.

It was early in the morning, and Conor had collected a package at Robinson's bookstore for Miss Martin. Miss Martin was a new teacher that had arrived at the school two months previously, and was very different from the other teachers at St Charles. She was a lot younger and had a very pretty face with silky, long blonde hair. The boy and the new teacher had hit it off straight away, and had long conversations about everything and anything. She wore brightly coloured clothes that were similar to his Aunt Claire, and in some ways the new teacher reminded the boy of his aunt. Conor had not seen Claire for six years now and he still missed her deeply. The rift between father and sister had deepened to the point that his father refused to talk about her, other than to say that she now lived in Scotland.

His other old friend Tom the caretaker had passed away just a few months ago, and he recalled the day it happened. The Third Form were in the classroom when they saw some activity outside around Tom's tool shed. People were coming and going, and soon an ambulance pulled up outside. The shed was a good distance away, so they could not see what was happening, but the ambulance left after a short while and disappeared through the school gates. There were rumours all around the school about Tom, and that he had died. The headmistress called the assembly together the following morning, and addressed the school with all the staff sitting on chairs behind her. She explained that Tom had died suddenly yesterday, of what appeared to be a heart attack, in his tool shed. She said that they would miss him terribly, and that he was a great colleague and friend to them all. Conor could see the teachers behind, some were looking very solemn and others were crying openly. Conor did not cry, but when he got home he went downstairs into the pub and picked up the little oilcan from its canvas bag and sobbed uncontrollably.

He still visited the pub downstairs every day and kept it ship shape. He had picked up an old soda siphon and a set of ashtrays from a stall in the Shepherd's Bush market. The soda siphon was placed on the bar counter, and the ashtrays on the tables around the place. The pub was still very much central to his day, and he always seemed to be at his happiest there. For a long period of time he had blocked out what happened in 1961, but every time he looked at Tom's bag with its little oilcan it brought it all back to him. The trauma of the whole episode was still held deep within him, which meant he had never been tempted to go through the door under the stage since.

His parents still worked in Askey's but the street had been devastated with job losses due to the recession. Two years previously the Tomasevskis had moved back to Poland, and just a few months later the Batemans to another part of London. All the way from his parents building to the canal was now just a row of empty houses. He remembered saying goodbye to the families as they left, and in particular Peter Tomasevski, who was very upset. The boy thought he had seen nothing sadder than the sight of the huge man crying.

The tube train rattled on. He loved the feel of the train as it raced from station to station. He went into London as often as he could, and Hyde Park Corner and Shepherd's Bush market on Saturday and Sunday were two of his favourite haunts. The tube was empty this morning, which was rare, and he got up off the seat and swung off the handles that hung down from the ceiling. He felt the fabric of the seats which was smooth in one direction and bristly in the other. The carriages always smelled of a mixture of stale perfume and cigarette smoke, but he loved travelling on them.

The annual trips to Ireland continued, and he looked forward to them less and less as he got older. He had a running battle with his father about the length of his hair, which he invariably lost when he was marched to Ken the barber before they headed off to Ireland. After these visits he emerged from Ken's looking like a refugee which the boy resented bitterly. His parents had told him recently that there would be no trip to Ireland this summer. They did not offer an explanation, and he did not seek one, but later he danced around the stage of the Portobello in celebration.

Summer holidays from school were now just two weeks away,

and he was looking forward to a great Ireland-free summer. The tube slowed and the signs for Ladbroke Grove flashed by the windows as the train squealed to a stop. Ladbroke Grove was an overground station and he loved the brightness of it. Along with Baker Street which was underground, it was his favourite station in London and he had visited many of them. As the doors opened with a swoosh, he jumped off the train with the package for Miss Martin under his arm, and skipped down the two flights of stairs in two bounds. As he passed the Cadbury's Chocolate bar machine on the way down the stairs, he saw Malcolm the station man at the exit barriers who said, "Hello, Conor, how are things?"

"Never ever better, Malcolm," said the boy as he handed the man his ticket.

They smiled at each other and the boy turned left out of the station towards St Charles Square.

Walking with a spring in his step he passed the Parish Church of St Michael, with its beautiful old red-brick facade, and the Tavistock Pub on Ladbroke Grove. The Tavistock stood on a corner, and he imagined that was exactly how the Portobello on Kensal Road must have looked when it was open. He turned down St Charles Square and saw the figures in grey spilling out through the gates of the school onto the foot path. As he passed through the gates, he saw her for the first time.

She was as tall as him and very skinny. Instead of the school uniform, she wore a short black dress with white edging and black leather boots. She had very dark and tightly cropped hair with a long fringe that hid her eyebrows. Her eyes looked like they were black rather than brown and almost seemed to be too big for her face.

He stopped in front of her and gave her a military salute.

She saluted back and said, "Melanie Allen."

"At ease, Melanie," he said and reached out to shake her hand in a formal way that made her smile. As they shook hands he said, "I am Conor O'Loughlin. I have not seen you here before. Is this your first day at the old barracks?"

"Yes, we have just moved to London from Brighton."

"What class are you in?" he asked.

"I am going into the Fourth Form next term."

"The same as myself."

She smiled at that and said, "Great! Do you always go around saluting people with a box under your arm."

He looked down at the box and said, "Oh God, always, yes." It was then that he saw Miss Martin standing beside them.

Gesturing with his free hand he said, "Miss Martin, Melanie – Melanie, Miss Martin."

The teacher shook hands with the girl and smiled. "Welcome to St Charles, and please ignore the barracks comment."

"Thank you, Miss."

"I expect that I will be taking you for English and Geography next term." The teacher turned to Conor, pointed to the box and said, "Will you put that into the staffroom for me, Conor?"

He saluted both the teacher and the girl, and saying "Miss, yes, Miss" he marched off with the box under his arm.

The girl and teacher both laughed as they watched him go and continued their conversation.

The teacher said, "I couldn't help but overhear. So, Melanie, how does it feel to be in London? It must be a big change from Brighton. Do you miss it?"

The girl looked at her and said quietly, "If I am really honest, the thing I miss most is the sea."

The teacher continued, "I expect this will be a big change for you, but if you need anything, please don't hesitate to let me know. I am fairly new to St Charles, but I have lived in London for quite a while."

The girl smiled and just said, "Thank you so much. I am looking forward to your classes next year, and I expect the summer will give me a chance to get to know London better."

Just then the bell sounded, and Miss Martin said, "Great to meet you, Melanie, and remember, if there is anything I can do please let me know."

She walked towards the staffroom, and as previously with Conor, she took to the girl immediately. Even though she had only spoken briefly with her, the teacher saw the same deep intelligence and character in the girl that she had already seen in Conor. She smiled and half whispered to herself, "Oh God, now there are two of them."

Chapter 8

The class schedule had been posted on the noticeboard in the hall, and it confirmed that Miss Martin would be taking the Fourth Form for Geography and English in the next term. It was Friday – the last day before the holidays – and the Third Form were waiting for Miss Martin. Earlier in the week she had pinned an invitation for a getting-to-know-you-session, with the added mystery of a summer project. A summer project was something that was not greeted with much enthusiasm by the youngsters, and there was an air of apprehension all about the classroom. On the top table was the box that Conor had collected in Robinson's bookstore.

Conor looked across the classroom at Melanie. Over the past two weeks, he had got to know the girl very well and they had become the best of friends. She challenged the boy intellectually, and he was delighted with the challenge rather than being resentful of it. He looked away when he saw Miss Martin entering the room. She stood at the top desk and addressed the class. "Hello I am Miss Martin and I will be taking you for English and Geography next year. What I want to do today is outline a summer project that I would like you to consider taking. It is not compulsory, but I believe if you do take it you will enjoy it, and it will help you to transition to the Fourth Form." The "not compulsory" comment lightened the mood of the youngsters considerably.

"There are twelve of you here, and I have maps for twelve of the major cities of the world." She pointed to a small box on the desk and said, "I have written the names of eleven of these cities on small pieces of paper, and you will each come up and draw a city. The city that you draw will be your project. There is one exception. Melanie, I am giving you London for your project as you are new here, but for the rest of you it is pot luck." She then wrote "London – Melanie" on the top of the board. The students went up one by one and pulled out a piece of paper. They called out the city and the teacher wrote it onto the board alongside their name. When Conor went up he picked out a piece of paper and looking at Miss Martin said, "New York." She smiled at him and wrote "New York" on the board with his name after it.

When the list was complete she said, "OK, so here is what I want you to do. I want you to plan and take an imaginary visit to your city. Part of your project is to write an essay about your trip. In this essay, I want you to describe your travel experience and the places you visited. The map will be your starting point, but I want you to go to the library also and explore the city from there. Take a look at its history and people, not just its geography. The first part of the project will be to write up your essay, and the second part will be a fifteen-minute presentation you will give to the class that expresses your opinion of the city's culture and society."

There was silence for a while and then a confused voice asked, "But how can we do that without being there, Miss?"

"You will have to use your imagination," she said. "For

any of you imaginary tourists that are going to take up the challenge, we will have two sessions for the presentations. The first session will be on the second-last Saturday before school term, and the second will be on the last Saturday. That will give us six presentations each day with some time for discussion. I have listed the day for your individual presentations, and as you can tell, I am very confident that all of you are going to take it on. We will start each of the presentation sessions at ten o'clock."

Conor looked around the class for reaction, and could hear the murmurings of approval all around. He could see that the teacher had managed to turn the normally indifferent group into a captive audience with her enthusiasm and passion.

"OK, class. That is the end of term."

She smiled and said, "All right you imaginary voyagers – don't let me down and class dismissed."

Conor bumped into Melanie in the playground as the school was emptying, and he said, "What do you think?"

The girl replied, "Of the project? I think it is great. I am really looking forward to it"

"When the projects were assigned I was just thinking that you are the only one that won't be an imaginary tourist," he said.

"Do you think it makes a big difference?" she asked.

"I don't know, but I expect we will find out at the end of the summer."

"When are you going to start looking around London?" he asked.

She looked at him and said, "As soon as possible." Then she paused. "Will you help me get to know the city?"

"Sure, no problem. When do you want to meet?"

She smiled and said, "We are going to Brighton this

weekend, and I will do a little work in the library there, so how about next Tuesday?"

"Great," said the boy.

"Ladbroke Grove Tube station at ten on Tuesday?" she said.

"Sounds like a plan," he said as they walked together up to the top of St Charles Square.

As they reached the top of the road she went right and he went left and she called back to him, "Tuesday at ten, Conor."

"Tuesday at ten it is."

Conor was sitting at the round table on the stage of the Portobello. It was early Saturday morning and he was killing some time before he headed into London. He was dressed in his denim jacket and beige cords. He had two favourite sets of clothes: a denim jacket with pale beige corduroy jeans, and a pale beige corduroy jacket with denim jeans. He always wore a fine, dark blue round-neck sweater with the denim jacket and a denim shirt with the corduroy jacket. He never mixed them around, and he always felt very comfortable in either combination. Above anything else, his most important clothing item was his pair of white sneakers with the blue stripes.

Conor had picked up a visitor's guide to New York that his father had in a drawer upstairs. The boy remembered some time ago asking his father about the guide, and he had told him that when he left the West of Ireland he was intent on going to New York, after spending a year or two in London. His father had told him that those plans all changed when he met the boy's mother.

The map of New York was open on the table and he was looking at the Island of Manhattan. He traced his finger southwards down along 5th Avenue to a patch of green in the south called Washington Square. He looked at the streets around the square and saw Waverly Place, Thompson Street. His finger froze when he saw Bleecker Street. Memories of 1961 came flooding back. He looked to his left and to the cut-out on the stage and shook his head in disbelief. "Hold on a minute ..." he said aloud with a very puzzled look on his face. He folded the map, put it into his pocket and thought, "I really need to think about this one ..." He left the Portobello, and went out the door of the building, heading towards Ladbroke Grove.

As he entered the station he went up to the window and said, "A daily ticket please, Malcolm."

"That will be sixpence."

The boy reached into the top pocket of his jacket, found a sixpence in his change and handed it to the man. Taking the coin, the man tore the ticket off a roll and handed it to the boy saying, "Here you go, Conor."

They smiled and the boy said, "Many thanks to yourself and the wonderful institution that is the London Underground."

"It is indeed our pleasure to serve you," said the man with a smile.

He took the train to Paddington Station, and then crossing Sussex Gardens he walked towards Hyde Park. Finding an empty park bench he sat down and thoughts started to come into his head. In the top pocket of his jacket was the visitors guide to New York. He did not know if the door under the stage of the Portobello opened out on to Bleecker Street in New York. It seemed like an explanation, albeit a completely illogical one. Browsing through the guide, he was pondering on whether he would dare try the door again. The first page had statistics, population, latitude, longitude, notable holidays and he saw that New York was five hours behind London. He looked at his watch and saw that it was eleven, so it was now six in the morning there. Every time he thought about giving the door another try, he felt a sickness in his stomach, and said to himself no. He wished he could talk it through with someone. Maybe he could discuss it with Melanie. Although he had not known her very long, he thought that she might understand. Having considered it for a while, he said to himself, "No, this is something that I need to decide."

He got up from the bench and walked towards Park Lane. The decision to go through the door or not go through the door was troubling him greatly. When he was making his way through the park he came across a fork in the path, and immediately remembered 'The Road Not Taken' by Robert Frost. His Aunt Claire had read the poem to him a long time ago, and told him if he never did anything else, he should learn it by heart as it would be his guide in life. He smiled at the memory, and the poem flashed before him and in particular the last verse:

> I shall be telling this with a sigh,
> Somewhere ages and ages hence:
> Two roads diverged in a wood, and I -
> I took the one less travelled by,
> And that has made all the difference.

He knew at that very instant, that whatever else happened, he was going through the door.

Chapter 9

He made his way back home and sat himself at the table on the stage. In front of him was a small torch and the canvas bag that Tom had given him years ago. He had decided that he was going to follow Tom's advice from before, and oil the lock before trying to open the door again. He lifted the door on the stage and made his way down the steps. Taking out the key, he poked the spout of the little oilcan into the keyhole squeezing it in and out until he saw the oil run down the door. Before he placed the key back into the lock, he squirted some oil onto it also. He wiped his hands with the cloth and placed all into the little canvas bag. Climbing up the steps he switched off the torch, then placed it with the little bag on the table. Looking at his watch he saw it was half past one, so he said to himself that he would give the door a try in half an hour. If it didn't open for him, he would add some more oil and leave it overnight. He jumped off the stage, sat up onto the bar and waited.

While he waited, he found himself thinking about Melanie. He could not quite understand what it was he was feeling, but it was not like anything he had felt before. It was a little disconcerting to him that he was waiting to see her next week at

Ladbroke Grove. He wondered what she was doing right now in Brighton, although he suspected she would be in the library reading up about London. He smiled, and thought: I bet that is exactly what she is doing.

He also thought about Miss Martin and the project. At this stage Miss Martin was as much his friend as his teacher, and he was very impressed at the ingenuity of the summer project. He could see the other students in the class were also very enthusiastic about it, which was a first for the Third Form in St Charles. New York City was something that really caught his imagination, and he was excited at the prospect of learning more about it. Miss Martin just seemed to have a gift for generating enthusiasm where previously there was none. He supposed it was her own passion for knowledge that she seemed to instil in those whom she taught.

He looked at his watch again, and it was five minutes to two. He said aloud, "not going to wait any longer." In three jumps he was on the stage, and with the bag and torch in his hand, he made his way down the steps. He gently took the key in his hand and tried to turn it. To his surprise it turned easily, and he opened and closed it a number of times, thinking: Good man, Tom. He removed the key, wiped it and put it back into the lock. Everything else was put into the little canvas bag and placed on the table.

He went to the door, took a deep breath and opened it. As he pulled the door towards him, the sunlight flooded the stairs under the stage. Locking the door behind him, he started up the steps and onto the street. It was exactly as he remembered it, and the first thing he saw was the sign "BLEECKER STREET". There were people walking to and fro, but unlike 1961 they all appeared to be relaxed. Some were carrying musical instruments, others had shopping in brown paper bags. They all seemed to be wearing brightly coloured clothes, and no two people were dressed the same. Although the street was very familiar, the atmosphere was not at all like he remembered. He was elated as he walked down the street, and he soon reached the point where Bleecker Street intersected with Thompson Street. He then stopped and looked all around him to take it all in. At that stage he knew that this was most definitely New York, and he did not care how or why this was so – he just wanted to experience it. To his left he could see some trees down at the end of the street, so he made his way in that direction. He was very careful to take a mental note of his surroundings, as the last thing he wanted was not to be able to find his way back again. At the bottom of Thompson Street was something that looked similar to a zebra crossing, but he noticed that the people were stopped instead of walking on to it. It was then that he spotted the illuminated red hand sign, so he waited with the people at the kerbside. Then the sign changed to green "Walk", and they all crossed the road together.

Directly in front of him were trees and shrubs, and up along the footpath to his right was a large opening into what looked to be a park of some sort, so he just followed the flow of people into it. It opened up into a large square with a big central fountain and an arch that reminded him somewhat of Marble Arch in London. As he passed into the square, he saw a sign on the railings saying "Washington Square". He immediately remembered the comment from the man in blue, "stay away from the square". He thought: I wonder was he referring to Washington Square.

As he walked through the square, there were lots of grassy areas with shrubs and pathways. People were walking to and fro or sitting on benches or on the grass. There was the sound of music in the air and he could see groups of people playing instruments. As he passed the fountain he headed towards the arch, picked out a bench at the end of a wide circle of benches and sat down. The arch was at his back, and he was looking back in the direction he had come. It was a much hotter day than in London, so he took his jacket off and placed it on his lap. He watched in awe of everything that was going on, and felt very much at home in this beautiful and relaxed place.

He must have been smiling, because he heard a gravelly voice beside him say,

"What are you smiling at?"

He had not noticed, but there was a man on the bench beside him. This was a rugged man, and the boy guessed he was in his sixties. Despite the warm weather, the man was dressed in cords with a grey wool jacket with the collar up and a blue peaked corduroy cap.

"I am sorry, I was miles away."

"You are not from around here are you?" the man asked.

The boy paused and said, "No I am from England – just visiting." There was silence for a while between the two.

"Are you from around here yourself?"

"No, just a visitor like yourself, from California originally."

"What do you do?" asked the boy.

"I am a writer."

"Are you a good writer?"

The man smiled and said, "What a fucking question!" and stuck out his hand and said, "John."

"Conor," said the boy and they shook hands. The boy looked closely at the man and saw beyond the rugged features to a pair of fierce steely-grey eyes. He looked like a man that was tough and uncompromising, but he also had an aura of calm wisdom that seemed to fill the space around him.

"Do you know this place well?" the boy asked.

"Yes, it is ingrained in me. I always seem to end up here."

"Why is that?"

"It is a place where change begins."

"What kind of change?"

"Change to culture, music, fashion – even to society." The boy and man looked at each other and smiled.

"Is that what you write about then?"

The man paused and said, "Sometimes the people I meet here end up as characters in my books."

"What do you do in England, then, Conor?"

"I go to school at St Charles in Kensington."

"Do you like school",

"Yes I do. This year I have a summer project to write up about New York."

The man looked at him and said, "Well this is a very good place to start – here in Greenwich. Where are you staying?"

The boy thought for a little and said, "Just off Bleecker Street."

"Great – a good spot to be."

The man rose from the bench and said, "I have to be getting back uptown. Are you here for the summer or just a short vacation?"

"For the summer I think."

"You don't seem to be sure."

"To be honest, I am not."

The man said, "Good day to you, Conor," and he started to walk away.

"Good day, John," said the boy.

The man stopped and turned around, "We might bump into each other again. I come here every morning about this time. So long."

"So long."

The boy knew immediately that he had to seek out this man again, and learn from him all about the place. Perhaps he could unravel the mysteries surrounding what happened in 1961. He watched as the figure in the grey coat and blue cap walked slowly out of the square, and up towards 5th Avenue.

Conor turned to look back at the people in the square. It was filled with music and laughter and he thought it was the most perfect place he had ever seen. He then thought to himself: I had better get back down Bleecker Street and into the Portobello. For a brief moment he panicked when he thought: God – what if I can't get back. He made his way down Thompson Street and turned onto Bleecker Street until he got to the steps and the black door at 248. He went down the steps, opened the door and pulled it closed behind him. He locked it and put the key into his pocket. When he had locked the door he paused for a moment, turned back and opened the door again. In front of him was the "BLEECKER STREET" sign, and he smiled as he closed the door and locked it again.

He went up onto the stage and pulled down the stage door. For a while he just sat at the small table trying to understand what he had just experienced. He asked himself: Was it real or was it a dream. He found it very difficult to overcome his need to understand how this was at all possible. It certainly felt very real to him, but he could not be sure. Eventually he concluded that it really didn't matter. What mattered was that he had the key and could use the door to visit New York whenever he wanted.

Chapter 10

It was Sunday morning and Conor was up very early. He was making a cup of tea when his father came into the kitchen. His father had on his navy blue overalls and was on his way to work.

"Are you working on Sunday?" the boy asked.

"Yes," said the father. He looked at the boy and anticipating the next question said, "Money is always a good thing to have you know."

"OK," said the boy.

His father asked, "What are you up to at the moment? We never seem to see you around lately."

"I am working on a school project."

"What is it about?"

"It is about the city of New York."

"Sounds like a good project."

"Yes, it is very interesting. I also have a friend that I am going to help with a project about the city of London."

The father paused for a little and looked at the boy. "OK, make sure that you work hard at it then." He reached into the pocket of his overalls, and handed him two half-crowns. "Your pocket money."

"Thanks," said the boy.

His father gave Conor five shillings each week, which the boy kept in the drawer of his bedside locker.

The boy's use for money was minimal, apart from the odd record or travel on the tube. He let the half-crowns accumulate, and when they had built up he would take them to the post office and exchange them for notes.

"Just a minute," said the father and he went back into the bedroom. When he came out, he handed the boy some bank notes. "These are some dollars that your Uncle Sean sent me from America. Maybe you can use them as part of your project."

"Great" said the boy.

As the father was leaving he turned back into the kitchen. It appeared to the boy that he was about to say something but then didn't; instead he just turned and walked out the door.

The boy hung around all morning. He wanted to go and visit New York, but he realised that it would be much too early, so he made himself a sandwich and a cup of tea. Apart from the odd breakfast with his mother, the boy looked after his own meals. This was very simple as the fridge in the flat was always packed with food. His mother made sure that meals were left for him and she would monitor if they had been eaten. After his sandwich, he made his way downstairs to the Portobello, where he read a little and wrote down some of his thoughts from the previous day's adventure.

At just a few minutes after two o'clock the boy was making his way down Bleecker Street. He had twenty-seven dollars in his pocket, and he was heading to Washington Square where he hoped to meet up with John the writer again. If he was not there, he was just going to wander around and try to familiarise himself with the place. As he entered the square, he spotted

John in the same place he was sitting the previous day.

He walked over to him and said, "Hello John."

"Hello, Conor, good to see you again," came the reply.

He sat down beside the man and looked around. The square was not as busy as it had been the day before. It was nearly deserted apart from some elderly people that were out walking their dogs. He tried to take it all in, and eventually he spoke, "This is a very peaceful place, has it always been like this?"

"How do you mean?" asked the man.

"I seem to remember someone telling me that there was a lot of trouble here a few years back."

"Oh, I suppose you mean the demonstrations over singing here in the square."

The boy sat forward and said, "Singing in the square?"

The man leaned forward and said, "Do you know the city tried to stop people singing here on Sundays?"

"When was this?" asked the boy.

"It was a few years back, in '61. The press called them the beatnik riots."

"What is a beatnik?"

"Well, the beatniks were the generation before this one and had their roots mostly in beat poetry, alternative art and jazz music. They were heavily influenced by free spirits like Jack Kerouac and Alan Ginsberg, and espoused individual freedom from right-wing ideologies. I suppose you could say they were like a post-war counter revolution."

The boy was transfixed by the man's words. "What is a right-wing ideology?"

"Do they teach you anything at school?" asked the man. "A right-wing ideology is a fascist notion of how society should be ordered – an extreme example would be Nazi Germany. These people believed – and still do believe – in racial supremacy.

They look to destroy anything that does not conform to their vision of an ordered society."

The boy could see that the man was very passionate about this, and there was fire in his eyes. The writer continued, "The people here are free to play their music on Sundays because of the efforts of the previous generation. They won the right to express themselves in music and song on Sundays. There was one glorious moment on a particular Sunday, when the protestors bested the authorities by singing the 'Star Spangled Banner'. This may seem to be a very small victory over a very small cause, but to me any threat to personal freedom should be fought against with passion and courage."

The boy thought for a while on what he had heard and said, "I am confused."

"How old are you, Conor?" the man asked.

"Fourteen," the boy replied.

"Why the fuck wouldn't you be confused?" the man said with a laugh.

Without diverting his eyes from the man, the boy said simply and clearly, "I don't want to be confused. I want to understand what motivates people to bring their notion of order to society."

The man looked at the boy and said, "Jesus, you don't want much, do you? I have been trying to do that for fifty years." He continued, "Every time I get close to some answers, a new generation comes along, society changes – and fucks up my project."

"Were the beatnik riots very violent?" asked the boy.

"The police were unnecessarily brutal in their treatment of the protestors. The city viewed the protests as a challenge to order, and I suspect it frightened them."

The boy kept watching the man's face throughout the

conversation. Eventually he said, "OK, I understand."

The man said, "Do you know what, Conor? I really believe you do."

They smiled at each other.

"What do you want to do when you finish with school?"

"I have absolutely no idea. I am only fourteen, you know," the boy said with a grin. They both laughed.

"You know what?" John said as they were laughing, "I reckon you are a bit of a smart-ass."

They were silent for a little while and John asked, "Do you always say exactly what you feel?"

"Yes, I have no time for small talk – it annoys me. I don't mind joking around, but talking about meaningless stuff is just a waste of energy."

John looked at the boy and said, "Good man, Conor. Don't ever change."

The boy looked at him and said, "Never."

They sat and watched the people in the square for a little while and John asked, "Have you ever visited the Guggenheim?"

"No," said the boy. "What's the Guggen– whatever you call it?"

John smiled and said, "It is a collection of art both contemporary and conventional. Do you want to see it sometime?"

"What? With you?" asked the boy.

"Don't make it sound like a fucking death sentence! You might learn something."

The boy laughed and said, "Is it far from here?"

"No, only about thirty minutes by subway uptown."

Conor thought about this for a little while and said, "How about tomorrow morning about this time?"

"Sure," said the man. "I will see you here at about ten o'clock. Just remember, when you go there, leave your preconceived ideas outside the door."

"Sounds like a fun trip," said the boy.

The man laughed, shook hands with the boy and walked off with a "see you tomorrow" over his shoulder.

The boy looked at his watch and it showed three o'clock. He thought: I had better keep my head about me or I could get mixed up very easily here. He strolled around the square and spotted a man on a bicycle with a large white container on the front. The man wore a white shirt and slacks with a red-and-white striped hat.

"Get your ice creams here at Giuseppe's. We got twenty different flavours."

The boy waved at him and he came over and said, "What can I get you today my young friend?"

"What have you got?" asked the boy.

The man kicked down a stand that was fitted under the bicycle, and pulled the bike up onto it. He lifted the lid up off the container in front, and there were tubs of ice creams placed neatly alongside each other. Stacked on one side were ice-cream cones.

The man said, "See, we got twenty different flavours at a quarter a scoop."

"What does that mean?" The boy asked.

The man had spotted the foreign accent, and picked up the steel scoop and said, "For every one of these, it will cost you one quarter of a dollar."

"OK," said the boy. "Do you have raspberry?"

"Sure do," said the man. "Do you want a scoop of something else with that?"

"OK then," said the boy. "I will have another scoop of raspberry."

The ice-cream man smiled at the boy and said, "I like a man that knows his own mind."

He caught the scoop and lifted the cover off one of the tubs, and pressed the scoop into it. He picked up a cone, and pulling a lever under the scoop he pushed a round scoop of the pink-coloured ice cream onto the cone. He repeated this again and handed it to the boy saying, "That will be fifty cents."

The boy reached into his pocket and picked out a single dollar and handed it to the man. Out of a leather purse around his waist, the man handed over two silver coins to the boy saying, "A pleasure doing business with you."

He pulled the bike back off the stand and cycled off again, calling, "Get your ice creams here at Giuseppe's — we got twenty different flavours."

The boy tasted the ice cream, and it was the best he had ever had. He ate it as he made his way over to the exit of the square, and onwards to the door on Bleecker Street. He had eaten his ice cream down to the cone when he noticed the cone had "Askey's" on the side of it. He laughed to himself and thought, How's about that, then? and he made his way back to the Portobello.

Chapter 11

C onor and the writer stood at the souvenir kiosk outside the Guggenheim Museum. They had just travelled up from Bleecker Street by subway. The boy watched out for the names of the stops as the two travellers made their way uptown, 23rd Street, Grand Central. He had studied the train route the evening before in the New York visitor's guide. The London Underground was very familiar to him, but the subway in New York had a completely different feel to it.

The train was not busy and he reckoned that this was because it was not rush hour in New York. John sat beside him watching the faces of the people that were coming and going. This is something that the boy also liked to do in the tube. The majority of people on the train in London avoided any eye contact, and it seemed that in New York it was exactly the same. If the travellers were not reading, they studied the train map over the windows. The boy figured that although trains may be different, people travelling in them must be the same all over the world. His conclusion was that the most crowded places are where the least amount of conversation is to be heard.

The kiosk carried all sorts of memorabilia. There were paper weights of the Empire State Building, American flags and round glass balls with scenes of New York that glittered with falling tinsel when they were shaken and turned upside down. There were postcards of New York and some of famous paintings. One of the postcards that caught the boy's eye was of a man and woman standing in front of a church, the man with a fork in his hand. John noticed the boy's interest in the postcard. He bought a few postcards and stuck them into the green khaki shoulder bag that he carried everywhere with him. They turned around and got into the queue for the museum that was forming behind them, and made their way inside. John bought two tickets at the booth and handed one to the boy.

Neither spoke as they went from painting to painting. Conor found himself becoming absorbed in the place. They went up a spiral walkway into the permanent exhibition, and stood in front of a painting of a man sitting on a chair. The name plate said, "PAUL CEZANNE – *MAN WITH CROSSED ARMS*."

They looked at it for some time, and at last John spoke, "What do you make of it?"

The boy thought about it and started to think out loud,

"It is a very simple painting of a man sitting in a chair, with his arms folded."

The writer said nothing but just let the boy continue.

"He is looking off into the distance."

"His folded arms seem like he is being defensive or that he does not want to be disturbed."

Conor continued looking at the painting and said, "Perhaps what he is looking at is making him uncomfortable, or maybe he does not want to look at whoever is painting him. Perhaps he is embarrassed by his looks, or he dislikes the painter."

John was looking at the boy closely but did not interrupt.

"There is a depth of knowledge etched in his face."

"I get the feeling that the man being painted could be the painter himself, so perhaps he is both the creator and the subject."

The boy shrugged his shoulders and said, "Or maybe he is just sitting on a chair with his arms folded looking into the distance."

There was silence for a while as the two stayed looking at the painting, and then they moved on. They spent an hour making their way around the other paintings in the permanent exhibition, but did not engage in any further discussion. Eventually they emerged back out of the museum and left the Guggenheim behind them.

The two were on the subway downtown after the visit to the Guggenheim, when John suggested they get off at 59th Street and go into Central Park. Having left the subway, they were now busily eating hotdogs that they had purchased from a stand at the entrance to the park. As they walked into the park, they passed the zoo and the clock, but neither were of any interest to them. It was a hot summer's day, and the smells in the air were of mustard, onions and manure from the horses that were queued up outside the park. When they bought the hotdogs from the street vendor, the boy was asked what he wanted on it. Conor looked a little confused, and John described the different toppings: onion, relish, ketchup and hot chilli. The boy opted for onions and tomato sauce as he chose to call it. They found a bench and continued eating. Conor thought it was good, but not as good as the chipolata sausages his mother used to cook for him at home. When they had finished their hotdogs, Conor took the wrappers and placed them into a nearby bin. The two sat back on the bench, and John lit up a cigarette. He took out the postcards from his bag and flicked through them. He stopped at the picture of the elderly couple and held it out from him, "American Gothic – painted by Grant Wood."

The boy leaned across, "Yes, I saw that on the stand."

"What do you see?" asked the man.

The boy took the postcard from the man's hand and held it in front of him. He must have been looking at it for several minutes and then said, "He is holding a fork in his hand in defiance, with the church at his back. The fork looks threatening, and he stares at the viewer in a fierce and uncompromising way that makes you fear him."

The boy paused and said, "The man and woman have a lean and sinewy look that says their life does not have much happiness."

He paused for another while and said, "She has a look of unspeakable sorrow and her eyes are directed away in the distance. Perhaps the man's uncompromising nature is the reason for her sorrow."

A troubled expression came on the face of the boy. "They are in front of a church which is where a graveyard might be, and maybe she is looking at the graves of people she knew."

He paused, drew a deep breath and said quietly, "I wonder if the graves are her children's." He handed back the postcard to the man.

John smiled at him and put the postcard back into his bag without a word. Conor asked, "Why do you look for my opinion on the paintings, and then not comment yourself?"

John said, "I am a writer and learning how people view things gives me fresh insights."

"Are you saying that you are learning from me?"

The man laughed and said, "In some ways, yes. You see things in a unique and intuitive way that has not been distorted yet by influences from education or media."

The boy said, "Are you saying education and media destroy the ability to understand?"

"Shit, what a question," and he smiled at the boy. "How can I explain this ... some forms of education that dictate an understanding that is aligned to certain moral or cultural ideals, can distort the essence of pure perception. Does that make sense to you?"

"Yes," said the boy.

The man said, "Conor, I believe that at your stage in life you have a clear and unbiased view, not just of art but of society in general."

They sat for a while without speaking. John said, "My time for writing is nearly done my young friend, but your time has not yet begun."

"Are you saying that I am going to be a writer?"

"I am saying that you may not have a choice," and he smiled at the boy.

The boy said, "I asked you before if you are a good writer, and you didn't answer me."

"Good is a bit of a subjective term, don't you think?"

"Perhaps," said the boy.

The man gave a little laugh and said, "People say I am good and I have sold many books but to me that means I am popular. There is a difference between writing that is valuable and writing that is of value. It will be a long time after I am gone when my work will be understood to be of value or not. The painting by Cezanne of the man with the crossed arms would be bought for millions, but that does not say that it has value."

"Do you think it has value?" asked the boy.

"What do you think?" said the man.

"Do you always answer a question with a question?" said the boy with a laugh.

"Pretty much," said the man.

The boy thought for a little and said, "The Cezanne painting made me think, therefore it has meaning or depth to me that is not visually obvious. In that regard, to me it has value."

They were silent for a while again, and Conor said, "Going back to what you said earlier, are you saying that my view of the world will have less value when I become influenced by formal education?"

John smiled. "Education is a wonderful thing, but if what you do in life is to have value, you cannot allow it to take away your uniqueness. Have you heard of the Spanish painter, Picasso?"

"Yes," said the boy.

"He is quite an old man now, and he has said that it has taken him all of his life to learn to paint like a child. Do you get it?"

The boy looked at him, smiled and said, "Yes."

They strolled back through the park and John pointed out the tall buildings that ran along the side of the park. He stopped up and pointing to the buildings said, "This is the Upper East Side of Manhattan, and over there is the Upper West Side. Apartments along here cost a fortune – sometimes millions of dollars. The key to the value of the apartment is a view of the park."

The boy said, "It is much the same in Park Lane in London."

The man turned to him and said, "I have stayed in Park Lane many times – at the Dorchester. Do you know it?"

"Yes", said the boy. "I pass by it sometimes on my way to Speakers' Corner."

"Are you going to get out your own soapbox, and give it a go?"

The boy looked at him and smiled, "Someday maybe."

They walked on and John said, "Let's head back to Greenwich. I get tired easily nowadays."

The boy could see the tiredness in him that he had not seen before, but the steeliness was still in the eyes. They walked together towards the park entrance and onward to the subway station on 59th Street.

Chapter 12

It was drizzling rain on Tuesday morning and Conor and Melanie were on the train from Ladbroke Grove to Paddington Station. Melanie wore a pair of jeans and a white blouse under a long, black, crochet- knitted coat that touched her knees. There were no sleeves to the coat, so it looked like a very long waistcoat. Conor had on his usual jacket and jeans. This time the combination was a corduroy jacket with denim jeans. Melanie told the boy everything about her trip to Brighton and he had been right – she had spent a lot of time in the library reading up about London.

When they met at Ladbroke Grove, Melanie had decided that she wanted to go to Hyde Park and then on to the Tate Gallery. They took the first train and in five minutes they were in Paddington Station. When they emerged out of the station onto Praed Street, the rain had stopped, and it was looking like it was going to be a fine day. They turned down towards Sussex Gardens and headed for the park. Rather than enter the park, they decided to walk down towards Park Lane.

Melanie spoke, "I realised when I was in Brighton, just how much more there is in London – I love it here," and she smiled at him.

He said, "I have never lived anywhere else – and I do love it too."

"Where is your favourite place in London?" She asked.

Without any hesitation and without knowing why he said, "My pub."

"Your pub?"

"Yes, there is an old pub in the ground floor under our flat that closed during the war. I found a way of getting into it, and I use it as a place to go – it even has a stage."

She said, "It sounds fantastic, what do you do there?"

Conor looked at her and said, "I read and write, study a bit, and sometimes I just sit and think."

"Will you show it to me some time?"

He was a little hesitant and she sensed this. "I am sorry, I did not mean to be pushy. I expect it is a private place for you."

He said, "No, I was a bit taken aback. You see, I have never spoken about it or showed it to anyone before, but yes, definitely, you must see the place."

She smiled at him and said, "Thank you I would love to see it."

At this stage they were on Park Lane and passing by the fancy car showrooms. As they continued, on their left was the forecourt of the Dorchester Hotel. She nudged him and said, "Come on, let's take a look inside."

He thought of John's comments about the Dorchester and said, "OK, you know I have never seen the inside of it."

They walked through the revolving doors into a magnificent lobby with marble floors and dark-wood furniture. The ceiling had gold paint ornamentation all over it and it oozed luxury and wealth. They were barely inside the door when a tall liveried man, wearing a top hat, came over to them and said, "Can I help you?" The way that he spoke made it sound more of a threat than a question. Before Conor could speak, Melanie looked at the man directly and smiling said, "No, we are really quite all right thank you very much." She was not impolite, but she managed to let him know in a friendly way that she was not going to be intimidated by him. She then passed him by, followed by Conor, and they entered the foyer. It was very clear that her poise and confidence made her fit right into the surroundings, and the tall liveried man had acknowledged as much and backed away.

They spent some time in the Dorchester. They looked into the dining room. She went to the Ladies and he to the Gents and were handed towels by the waiting attendants. Eventually they found their way back out onto Park Lane and resumed their stroll. Cutting across the road, they entered the park and found a bench where they could sit and chat. He looked at her and thought to himself that everything about her radiated energy and confidence.

She caught him looking and said, "Do you get tired of London?"

"No, I always learn something new. Take today for example, I got to see inside the Dorchester."

She smiled and said, "When I see a sign saying, 'Private Property Keep Out', or someplace that sets itself out to be exclusive, I have to go in."

He smiled back at her and said, "I'd hate to try and stop you."

She giggled and punched him playfully on the arm.

They sat for a while and she asked, "What do you want to do when you leave school?"

He said, "I have absolutely no idea. You know I was asked that by a friend of mine recently, and I gave him the same answer."

"OK, what about college then?" she said.

"My friend said to me that at this moment in my life I have

a unique and unbiased perception, and warned me not to let formal education corrupt or influence that view – ever."

She had gone very serious and said, "That is very profound, but is he anti-education?"

"No, he is not against education – he thinks it is a wonderful thing, but his warning is not to let it bias your own understanding. I suppose bad educators sometimes get you to think like them and not like yourself."

The girl asked, "What does your friend do?"

"His name is John and he is a writer," said the boy.

She looked at him excitedly and said, "Do you think I could meet him?" She immediately looked away and said, "Oh God, that is me being pushy again. I am so sorry."

The boy looked at her and said, "Don't be sorry. I think it is a great idea. Just let me think about how I could make it happen."

She asked, "What is his second name? Maybe I have read something by him."

Conor paused for a moment before he spoke. "This may sound a little strange, but I do not want to know until he wants to tell me. You see, I suspect that he is quite a famous author, and knowing his work might change the way we engage with each other. A bit like knowing of him rather than knowing him, if you get what I mean. We have not discussed this, but I am fairly certain that would be his view too."

She smiled and said, "I understand. You know something – you are in real danger of becoming my hero."

He said nonchalantly, "But of course."

"Do you want to go and get a cup of tea?" she asked.

He said, "Only too delighted, my dear. Let's find the perfect place for a perfect cup of tea."

As they walked along, he asked, "What do you want to do

when you finish with school?"

Without any hesitation, she replied, "Journalism."

"You seem to be very sure."

"I had a friend who was the editor of a paper, and she was a huge influence on me. I have known since the day I first met her that is what I wanted to do. By the way, and in case you have not noticed, I can be quite opinionated." She smiled at him and said, "I do not have any doubts that journalism is what I want to do."

He looked at her and saw the steeliness that he had seen in John. They walked out of the park and onto Park Lane, and he said, "It's great to be fourteen."

She smiled at him.

On a side street off the lane, they spotted a small coffee shop and they made their way through the door. Inside there were rows of red Formica tables, and the chairs were covered with red plastic. On each table was a cluster of red and brown sauce bottles, salt and pepper, a stainless steel jug of milk and a large jar of sugar with a spout. There was a smell of fried bread and sausages in the air, and the area behind the counter was partly hidden in a fog of steam. They went to the counter, and a tall lady with a white coat and turban asked, "What would you like?"

Conor looked at the girl and she said, "Tea."

"Can I have a tea and a foamy coffee with toast?"

"Is that two rounds of toast or one?"

Again he looked at the girl and she said, "OK."

"Two," he said to the lady.

The lady in the white coat said nothing, but pulled out a tray from under the counter. In a blizzard of movement, she had it filled with a small pot of tea, a cup and saucer, a mug of coffee, a rack with slices of toast with some butter and a dollop of red jam on a small dish.

"One and thrupence," she said, and Conor handed her a two shilling coin. The lady rang up the till and placed the change on the tray. She did not say thank you or anything, but just turned away to do something else. She was not rude or unfriendly, and in a funny way the boy felt it was a bit like being at home. They found a table in the corner and the boy placed the contents onto the table and brought the tray back to the lady at the counter. Again she did not speak, but just took it, nodded, and in one movement, wiped it with a cloth and placed it under the counter.

They sipped their drinks slowly, and munched on the toast. Melanie asked, "What do you think of Miss Martin?"

"I really like her. She is very different to the other teachers. What do you think of her?" he asked.

"I think she is great. I would like to know what she thinks of the educational system. I expect her views would be quite radical. For example, getting us to do this city project is quite different. How is it going with New York, by the way?"

"Good," the boy said, "I am getting a lot of insights from John."

"Does he know New York well?

"Yes, he is an American and spends a lot of his time there," the boy said thoughtfully.

They sat in silence for a while. A wheezy old man went over to the jukebox in the corner, put some coins in the slot and selected a few songs by pressing down on the keys at the front. He turned and sat down, and the discs inside the machine spun and then stopped. An arm reached down, picked up the disc and placed it on the turntable. 'Waterloo Sunset' started to play and the two sat and listened to the music.

As the song was nearly over Conor said, "OK, 'Julie', do you want to do the Tate?"

"OK," she said, and they left the café to the strains of Waterloo Sunset's fine.

Chapter 13

The boy and girl sat on a long bench in the Tate Gallery. They had travelled by tube to Pimlico which was the closest station, and had made their way to the gallery. They were looking at Dod Procter's painting, *Morning*. This was a quiet part of the gallery with some lesser-known works on display. The more famous paintings had crowds of visitors crammed in front of them, and the two were happy to sit and chat in this less crowded part of the gallery.

Conor said, "I love to come in here and sit in front of this painting."

"Why this particular one?" She asked.

"I don't know – I just find her so peaceful."

"I know what you mean."

They were quiet for a while, and then she said, "I think this summer is going to be special."

"In what way?" he asked.

"I don't quite know. I suppose moving to London has been a big change for me."

Alongside the painting by Dod Procter was a very simple pencil sketch by Picasso, of an old man sitting in a chair.

Conor saw her looking at it and said, "You know that Picasso has said that it has taken him all of his life to learn to paint like a child."

"How do you know all of this stuff?" she asked.

He simply said, "John."

They had been sitting quietly for about ten minutes when she said, "Do you mind if we walk back to Ladbroke Grove instead of getting the tube?"

"It is a bit of a walk, you know, must be nearly five miles."

"OK," she said, "if we start off walking we can always get a tube or bus if you get too tired." As she said this, she smiled in a mischievous way.

"I see that the gauntlet has been thrown down. OK, I take up the challenge."

As they walked through the gallery, they came upon the painting by Sargent of Ellen Terry as Lady Macbeth.

Melanie stopped and said, "Lady Macbeth from the play."

Conor asked, "Do you like Shakespeare?"

"Oh, God yes. Do you know that is the crown of King Duncan that she is holding over her head?"

"Have you seen the play?" asked the boy.

"Yes, but it was the film version with Orson Welles as Macbeth and Jeanette Nolan as Lady Macbeth. I saw it with my parents in Brighton."

"What did you think of it?"

She laughed and said, "I was only ten and it frightened the life out of me."

They left the gallery and went out through the Tate's huge doors and down the steps towards the Thames. They crossed the street and looked at the Thames for a little while.

Conor said, "Dirty old river."

The girl smiled at him and said, "That song seems to be the

theme for the day, doesn't it?"

They crossed back over the street and turned onto Marsham Street and then along by Vincent Square. They chatted as they walked, and stopped now and then to look at some of the old buildings that they passed. When they got close to Hyde Park, he stopped up and asked her, "Do you want to take a break and sit by the Serpentine?"

"What is the Serpentine?"

"It is a lake that is in Hyde Park."

She smiled and said, "That sounds lovely – Lay on Macduff."

Conor guided them through the park until they eventually came to the lake. It had turned out to be a warm sunny day and around the park was quite crowded with little children everywhere in swimsuits, paddling in the water. There were people in rented timber boats, some were rowing and others just drifting along. At one side of the lake was a cluster of deckchairs, and this seemed to be where most of the activity was centred.

They found a spot under a tree and sat on the grass soaking in the atmosphere. Conor was resting on his elbow and turned to the girl, "What was it like living in Brighton?"

She looked at him and said, "I love the sea and the shops in The Lanes of the old town. The piers are beautiful too, especially when they are lit up at night."

She pursed her lips and continued, "There was a lot of trouble there with the Mods and Rockers." She held her hands to her head and said, "God I hated that so much – idiots with their mindless violence."

She turned to the boy and smiled when she said, "I really loved school there though. I had a great teacher, Mr McCarthy who taught me English. He was a big influence on me."

She looked away from the boy, and he could sense a little sadness in her voice when she said, "Both Mr McCarthy and Sandra."

"Who is Sandra?"

"She was the editor of the local newspaper that I told you about, who was a friend to me growing up."

She looked up at the boy and said with a smile, "I will tell you the story someday."

They were quiet for a little while and she asked, "How about you then in London?"

He looked at her and said, "I love London, I love St Charles, I love all of it."

The girl said, "I got the right guide for my project, didn't I?"

"The very best," said the boy.

He paused for a little while. "I have lived in London all my life, but both of my parents are Irish, and we go there each summer for a holiday."

"What is it like in Ireland?"

"It is very different for me – I am used to the city and travelling on the tube. Ireland, with the exception of Dublin, is very rural. I find the people very friendly, but it does not feel like home for me in the same way as it does for my parents." He looked at her and said, "Do you get what I mean?"

She nodded, "Are you going there this summer?"

The boy beamed and said, "No."

They sat in silence for a while just watching the little children splashing and paddling in the water. There were a group of men on the other side of the lake that had some large model boats. The boats were very intricate and beautifully crafted. They had small engines and were steered by remote control. Each one of the boat owners had a box on a strap around their neck, with dials and a long telescopic radio antenna. They manoeuvred the boats very skilfully and would spend hours in their spots by the lake.

The air was filled with a very distinctive smell from the boats engines, which the boy likened to the smell of vinegar on hot fish and chips. You could hear the high-pitched whine from the boats' engines all around the lake.

He looked at the girl and asked, "Do you feel hungry?"

She said, "I do actually," as she looked at her watch. "You know, it is four o'clock."

"Let me get us a sandwich," he said.

"No, I will get them – what do you want?"

"Anything at all," he said.

The girl went up to the shop and came back with a ham and cheese roll, two bags of crisps and two bottles of Coke with straws. She handed him a bottle and a bag of crisps and sat beside him on the warm grass. She took the roll, tore it in half and handed a piece to him. They opened their bags of crisps, found the little blue bag of salt and sprinkled it over the contents. It was nice in the shade of the tree, and they took their time eating their food and drinking the cold drink. When all was eaten, Conor gathered the bottles and packages and placed them in the bin by the shop.

The boy came back and sat back down on the grass. Melanie pulled up her knees under her chin, looked at him and smiled. "Isn't this a perfect day?"

"You know what? It is," he said.

She looked down at her shoes and asked, "Do you go out with girls much?"

"Not really," he replied.

"Why is that? Have you not been asked?"

He turned and looked at her, and with his finger pointing

to his chin said, "Are you serious? Have you not noticed this face at all?"

She laughed out loud saying, "You really have a deep lack of self-confidence, don't you?"

"Yes," he said smiling, "How very kind of you to notice."

They were silent for a while and then he asked, "How about you?"

"How about me, what?" she said.

"Do you go out with boys much?"

"Not really either. I find that boys of my own age have nothing in common with me – boring little monsters the lot of them," she muttered.

He squinted at her and said, "Thanks for that one by the way."

She smiled and said, "I didn't mean you. I find you enigmatic."

"I am a bit of a puzzle then?"

"Yes, a bit."

"A bit of a puzzle, and not a boring little monster?"

He looked away from her and repeated, "A bit of a puzzle."

They smiled at each other and she said, "You are right, you know?"

"About what?" he replied.

"It is great to be fourteen."

Chapter 14

On one of his daily excursions to New York, Conor and the writer were sitting in the lobby of the Waldorf Astoria Hotel. They had taken the subway up from Greenwich as far as 51st Street. Facing them in the lobby was an ornate four-faced clock, and the entire place felt exclusive and expensive. The staff greeted John in a familiar way and the boy commented, "This doesn't seem to be your kind of place."

"You are right. It is not really my favourite spot."

"The staff here seem to know you. Do you spend a lot of time here?"

"From time to time I attend functions here for the literary community in New York."

"What are they like?" asked the boy.

"The literary community?"

"Yes," said the boy.

"They are by far and away the greatest bunch of assholes that have ever walked the planet."

"Why go then?"

"My agent makes me."

They were interrupted when a lady excused herself and

handed John a book, asking if he would sign it. John looked both annoyed and embarrassed, but he signed it inside the cover and said, "Thank you," handing it back to her.

"Does it bother you when people do that?" the boy asked.

"I find it excruciating," said the man.

They were silent for a while and a waiter in a white waistcoat came over to them. He addressed John and asked, "Will sir be dining with us today?"

John replied, "No, but sir would kill for a Jack Daniels with lots of ice."

"Very good, sir." The waiter turned to the boy and asked, "And for sir?"

"Coca Cola, please."

"Very good, and will sir be wanting ice with that?"

"Yes, please."

"Very good. I shan't be a moment." And with that he ghosted away.

After a while the boy looked at John and raising his eyebrows said, "God, what a performance."

The writer smiled and asked, "What do you think of the place?"

The boy looked around him and said, "It is very grand, and I suppose it gives you a sense that somehow you are important."

"In what sense important?"

"It sort of makes you feel that you are superior. Even the way the waiter calls you sir makes you feel that you are his better."

"Why do you think he wants to make you feel that you are better than him?"

"I expect, to justify the costs that go along with somewhere like this – so I suppose instead of just Coke with ice, I am getting a shot of superiority with it."

The man laughed and lit a cigarette.

The waiter arrived back with a tray held over his head. He laid down two white place mats onto the table and put a short, cut-glass tumbler filled with amber liquid and ice in front of John. In front of the boy was placed a tall glass full of ice, and the waiter poured the Coke into it. Because there was so much ice, he could only get half of the contents of the bottle in, so he left the half full bottle beside the glass. From his tray he took a silver serving plate that consisted of three separate bowls. In the bowls were green olives, cashew nuts and small wafer-type biscuits. When he had finished he just said, "Sirs", and ghosted off again. The two raised their glasses and said, "Cheers", and sipped on their drinks.

The boy looked at the writer and said, "What intrigues me more than this place and the waiter, is the lady getting you to sign her book."

John smiled, "I was wondering when you were going to get around to that."

The boy thought for a while and said, "It is the price that you pay for what you do, isn't it? And that is why you hate doing it."

The man laughed, "God, you can be a royal pain in the ass at times."

The boy smiled at the man and said, "It is my job."

They finished their drinks and John said, "I am feeling a little peckish, do you fancy some Chinese food?"

"What, here?"

John shook his head and said, "Fuck, no way! Let's head to Chinatown."

"There is a Chinatown in New York?"

"Yes, and I happen to be friends with a Chinese family that run a restaurant there, and they serve the finest Chinese food you will get anywhere."

John took the leather folder that the waiter had left on the table, shoved a few dollars into it and placing it back on the table said, "Let's get a cab."

With that, the two left the Waldorf behind them and went out through the revolving doors and onto Park Avenue.

The cab dropped the two off on Mott Street, and as they got deeper into Chinatown, Conor felt that he was no longer in New York. Even the street signs had Chinese characters as well as English. John guided him down a street that was teeming with people all talking in what he guessed was Mandarin. The aroma of roasted garlic hung in the air, and the smell along with the sounds of Chinese gave an "otherness" to the place.

They walked past restaurants that had rows of roasted ducks in the window that were a golden brown colour. Unlike other roasted birds that the boy had seen, these were complete with their necks and beaks and even their feet. They glistened with a sheen that told you they were succulent and crispy. They arrived at a small place that was not as brightly lit or as posh as some of the others, and John pointed to the sign over the frontage. It said "The Cantonese Palace", and in small letters "Proprietors: Jim and Molly Wang".

John said, "Here we are," and he stepped through the door and was followed by the boy.

Inside there were a few people eating at some tables, but it did not look anything special. A grey-haired Chinese man in a white coat came out from behind the counter with a broad grin that showed at least three gold teeth.

He said, "John, my friend", and with that he caught the writer's hand with both of his, and pumped it rapidly up and down.

He called out, "Molly, look who's here."

Out through the door from the kitchen came a round-faced Chinese woman also in a white coat. She was very petite with jet-black hair in a tight bun. When she saw John her face lit up.

She said, "Mr John, you are back." She reached out and hugged the man around the waist.

John bent down and kissed her lightly on the cheek.

The Chinese man asked, "Are you going to eat with us, John?"

"Yes, we will have some of your dim sum if that is OK, but first let me introduce you to my friend here, Conor." He turned to the boy and said, "Conor, these are my good friends Jim and Molly Wang."

They both shook the boy's hand in turn and welcomed him to the Cantonese Palace, and then led them both to a table near the front window.

Jim barked out something in Chinese, and a beautiful young Chinese girl in a long, white, silk dress emerged from the kitchen. The dress was very tight and had a long slit on one side. She smiled at John and shook him by the hand.

She then asked in an American accent, "What would you both like to drink?"

John asked for a beer, Conor ordered a coke and the girl left them to get the drinks.

Jim and Molly disappeared into the kitchen, and John turned to the boy and said with a smile, "I have been coming here for a long time." The girl in the white dress brought a tray with their drinks. She placed them in front of them, smiled and left them alone. The boy sensed that John was very much at ease here, and he asked, "How did you first meet Jim and Molly?"

"Oh, it must be about twenty-five years ago. I was just strolling around Chinatown, looking for somewhere to eat."

He turned and pointed to the door and said, "I bumped into

Jim standing in the doorway just over there."

"I asked him if his food was good, and he just looked at me and said the best Chinese food in the whole world. With that, I couldn't resist, and it has just developed from there. The girl that served us is their daughter Jasmine and I remember the night she was born."

He just looked at the boy and said, "Jim and his family are a good New York story."

Conor found out that dim sum was traditional Cantonese food in small bite-sized pieces. Jim and his wife brought out the food in small straw baskets. John knew all of the dishes, and as they sampled each, he told the boy the name and what it was made from. The boy tried all, but his favourite was Har gow, which was made from shrimps. They drank green tea with the food and Jasmine made sure that they were topped up. Jim and Molly alternated sitting with the two and the conversation flowed. The boy had never seen the writer more at ease, and it was clear that there was a strong bond between John and the Wang family.

When they had finished, Jim asked the writer, "When are you going to come over to the house."

"Maybe for New Year," said John.

"That is not until the end of January – too long."

"What year is this then, Jim?" asked the writer.

"This is sheep, next monkey."

Jim turned to the boy and asked, "What year you born?"

The boy replied, "1953."

"What month?"

"April."

"Snake – very lucky sign. Jasmine is snake too."

John looked at the boy and said, "The Chinese Zodiac is made up of twelve different animals, and the year you are born determines what sign you are. But remember, it is the Chinese year you are born which is calculated from the moon's cycle, and is not January the first, so New Year occurs every year in either January or February."

Jim said, "Years are Rat, Ox, Dragon, Monkey, Dog, Goat, Snake, Pig, Tiger, Horse, Rabbit, Rooster."

He pointed to the boy and said, "Your best match is Rooster, Snake."

He called out to Jasmine in Chinese and she gave the boy a piece of laminated paper with the dates for the Chinese New Year and the relevant animal signs. It went back to 1930 and forward to 2020.

The boy traced his finger to 1953 and said, "So the New Year's date in 1953 was the fourteenth of February."

"Yes," said Jim.

The boy asked, "You said my best match is Rooster and Snake – what does that mean?"

Jim smiled at him and just said, "Girl for you."

"OK," said the boy and he traced his finger along and read out, "1953 and 1957 are good, and the closest to my age. What about girls born in the other years?" he asked.

"For Snake, you avoid Tiger, Pig."

The boy looked at the paper again and said, "So I need to avoid a girl that is born in 1947 and 1950."

"Yes," said Jim.

"Did you consult this before you married Molly?"

"Yes, she is Dragon and I am Rooster."

"Is that a good match?" asked the boy.

"Yes, very good."

"If she was not Dragon would you have married her?"

"If she was Dog – no, if anything else, yes."

Jim smiled at the boy and said, "I can see why you are John's friend."

They finished off their tea and said their goodbyes to the Wang family. They left after much protest as the Wangs did not want payment, but John made sure that money was left. The writer also had to promise that he would visit the Wang home. Eventually John and the boy made their way up Mott Street where they hailed a taxi and it took them towards Greenwich.

John asked, "Where can I drop you?"

"Anywhere near the square."

As the taxi was pulling up at the square the boy looked at the man and simply said, "Great people."

John smiled at him and said, "Great people for sure – New York at her very finest." He raised his thumb and said, "See you tomorrow, Conor." The boy raised his thumb in reply and closed the door of the taxi behind him.

Chapter 15

Conor's summer had taken on a distinctive pattern. His mornings were spent in London with Melanie, and his afternoons were spent in New York with John. This meant that he had effectively two mornings – one in London and one in New York. He loved the time spent with John, and he looked forward to their treks around New York enormously. The mornings with Melanie were becoming more and more special to him. He felt so comfortable around the girl, to the point that they always seemed to be in step when they walked.

On this particular Friday morning, he was with Melanie in Shepherd's Bush market. They had just travelled the short journey by tube from Ladbroke Grove. The boy loved the market, and he made a point to visit it every week. The place had very distinctive smells, which were a mixture of musk and patchouli oil with fish and chips and that musty smell you got from old books. Melanie had read up on the market and wanted to explore the place further, and the boy was looking to buy some records. The vendors that ran the various stalls in Shepherd's Bush were different to other markets in London, they were mostly young and wore modern fashions. These younger stall owners gave the place a different atmosphere – more colourful and vibrant somehow.

As they strolled into the market, the two youngsters stopped at a stall that sold leather goods. It was full of bags and wallets and it even had some leather hats and a saddle. As she was checking out the stall, Melanie spotted a black leather shoulder bag that she liked. The man that ran the stall was tall and thin with shoulder-length, curly, red hair. His eyes were hidden behind small round glasses, and the lenses of his glasses were an inky blue colour.

She held up the black bag and asked, "How much?"

He replied, "They are beautiful, aren't they? Those ones are ten shillings and sixpence."

"Very expensive, isn't it." The girl made it a statement rather than a question.

"They are handcrafted by an artist friend of mine up in North Wales, and I only have that one left. I had six of them and they have sold out since this morning."

The girl held up the bag and looked at it carefully. "It is pretty, but I can't afford ten shillings and sixpence."

The man looked at her and asked, "What can you afford?"

"Eight shillings and sixpence."

He held out his hand to take the bag from her and said, "The leather costs more than that love."

She handed it back to him and she just shrugged her shoulders and said, "Pity."

As she was walking away, the man in the stall said, "Ten shillings and thrupence."

She stopped and turned to him saying, "Eight shillings and sixpence."

He muttered under his breath and said, "All right, ten shillings, and that is my final offer."

She looked at him and said, "Eight shillings and sixpence."

"I can't sell it for eight and six – I would be shot."

She shrugged her shoulders and started to move away.

As she was almost gone, he called out and said, "All right, but I am losing money here."

She came back and he handed her the bag. She counted out the eight shillings and sixpence, saying, "Thank you."

She put the bag over her shoulder and strolled on to the next stall.

Conor watched this performance closely, and he was very taken with how the girl had dealt with it.

He said, "You did pretty well back there."

She looked at him and said, "Not really – I bet you when we go back there again, there will be another bag the very same hanging up. And they are made in India, not in North Wales. It is just a bit of a game really, but I really liked the bag."

He smiled to himself and said, "Will we splash out the two shillings that you saved, and get a cup of coffee?"

She smiled back at him and said, "OK, Conor, the coffees are on me, or the guy with the blue glasses, depending on how you want to look at it."

In the centre of the market there was a coffee shop that was like a little straw hut with drop down sides. In the middle of the hut were the coffee makers and steamers. The girl behind the counter had very long and very straight, jet-black hair. She wore a black vest over a very short miniskirt with black tights and heavy black boots. He ordered a coffee for himself and a tea for Melanie, and the boy paid the girl behind the counter one shilling. This was done after much protest from Melanie, as she wanted to pay for the drinks. Conor brought the drinks down on a tray to a vacant table and set them out.

As they were sitting down to have their drinks, Melanie said to him, "I will get very mad at you if you don't let me pay my share you know."

She took out a shilling from her pocket and placed it on the table in front of him.

He looked at her and down at the coin and said, "One and six."

The girl burst out laughing, "God, you are incorrigible."

He smiled at her, took the shilling and put it into his pocket and said, "It is OK, you can owe me the sixpence."

She looked at him and narrowing her eyes said, "Don't push your luck, Conor. You are dealing with forces you can't comprehend."

The boy stared at her and the cup of coffee in his hand started to tremble.

She narrowed her eyes and said to him, "That's right, be afraid."

They were silent for a little while and she said, "You know, you are a great guide to London, in fact you may even get a special mention in my review." She continued, "My opening line will be, the first step to discovering London is to find a Conor."

The boy said, "Any Conor?"

"God yes," she said, "they are everywhere." And she gestured with her hand around the market.

She smiled at him warmly and said, "Well maybe not quite everywhere."

He smiled back at her and said, "It is no good you know – I still want my sixpence."

After a little while she asked, "Do you get tired of showing me around – It is OK if you do, I won't be offended."

"Not at all," said the boy. "In fact I really enjoy it. In some ways it gives me a fresh perspective."

"That is interesting, I did not think of it in that way."

SONGS *and* PORTOBELLOS

"You seem to forget – I am an enigma."

She laughed, "I am going to regret saying that, aren't I?"

"Oh yes, you will."

She asked, "By the way – and you can tell me to mind my own business – but what do you do in the afternoons? I only seem to see you in the mornings."

He thought for a little, and just said, "I spend the afternoons on my New York project."

She said, "God, of course. I was so wrapped up in my project, I forgot about that. How is it coming on?"

"Great. I am having good fun with it."

They sat and chatted for a while and then she asked, "Do you want to be getting back now, or do you want to look around some more?"

"I would like to pick up an LP here before we go," he said.

"OK," she said, "Let's go and get that, and then we can head back to LG after that."

"What's LG?" And then he immediately thought of it and they both said "Ladbroke Grove" together.

The two were standing in front of rows and rows of LPs, and Conor was flicking them down one by one so he could see the covers. He was not sure of what it was he wanted and he paused on Bob Dylan, the Cream and Gordon Lightfoot. He stopped flicking when he saw *The Paul Simon Songbook*. He had heard of Simon and Garfunkel and liked them a lot, but he did not know that Paul Simon had a solo LP. He turned it over to look at the track listing. He liked 'the Sound of Silence', 'Homeward Bound' and 'Kathy's Song', so he decided to buy it. This time it had a price tag of two pounds and five shillings. He looked at Melanie and said, "Do you think you can do your magic here?"

She laughed, saying, "I wouldn't even bother trying."

He handed over the two pound notes and two half-crowns to

someone that looked like the twin brother of the guy with the blue glasses at the leather stall.

The girl asked to see the LP and she said, "I like this too. Who are the two on the cover?"

He said, "The guy is Paul Simon, and I am not sure who the girl is."

She looked at the track listing and read the notes and handed it back to him.

They strolled around a little more and she stopped at the perfumes. The stall was full of little bottles and she opened some of them and sniffed the little glass stoppers. She did not buy any and as they moved on he asked, "Did you not like any of them?"

She said, "I find fragrances like musk to be too strong. By the way, and for your information, I wear Intimate by Revlon."

"Is that good?"

She laughed and said, "What a strange question."

"I would say enigmatic, not strange." the boy said with a smile.

She linked his arm and said, "OK then, let's get back to Ladbroke Grove."

Chapter 16

Over the course of the summer the boy and girl had trekked all across London. They went on a tour of Westminster and picnicked on Hampstead Heath. They had seen the changing of the guard, and sat near Tyburn where people were hanged in the Middle Ages. In just a few short weeks, they had shared wonderful days together and had become inseparable. As he got to know her more, he found that she was not just determined but fearless in everything she did. They used to meet up each morning at ten o'clock and he looked forward to the day's adventures with great anticipation.

When he was in New York, John was his mentor and guide. He had learned much from the man, but everything he learned stemmed from his own imagination and perception. Not once did the man impose his own ideas or beliefs on him. On the boy's daily visits, they had visited the New York City Library and went as far north on the Island as Harlem and down to Battery Park in the south. A lot of their time, however, was spent in Washington Square and around Greenwich Village.

On this day in August, the man and boy were sitting in their usual spot in the square.

"What was it like growing up in California, John? Is it nice there?"

"Beautiful," said the man.

"Why did you leave?"

"For me, travelling is a necessary part of the job."

Conor looked at him and asked, "Where is your favourite place?"

"That changes over time, but I have always loved this part of New York."

The boy had noticed in the last few weeks the man was looking older and moved more slowly. He said to him, "You look tired. Is there a problem with your health?"

John smiled at him and brushed it off with, "Fucked up from cigarettes, alcohol and women. How about a cup of coffee?"

"Sure," said the boy.

"OK then, let me introduce you to my friend, the Preacher."

The two left the square and strolled down Bleecker Street. They stopped at a bar and John pointed up to the sign over the door, in large gold letters it said "The Preacher".

When they went inside John told him, "This used to be a bible shop run by two old ladies, now it sells booze and coffee to agnostics like me."

"What is an agnostic?" the boy asked.

"An agnostic is someone who is firm in their belief that there is not a God but still likes to keep their options open about it."

The boy smiled and said, "It sounds like it could be a belief of convenience."

John smiled to himself and said, "You are not wrong."

There was a man behind the bar cleaning glasses, and immediately when he saw John he grinned and reached across the counter with his hand outstretched, "John, my friend, how are you?"

"Not bad, Tony. How is business?"

"It has been a great summer so far. Who is your young friend?"

"This here is Conor. He is visiting from England."

"Pleased to meet you, Conor." He spread out both his arms to either side of him and said, "I am the Preacher."

The boy guessed that Tony was in his late thirties. He was a very tall handsome man, and when he smiled he showed a set of the whitest teeth the boy had ever seen.

John asked, "Can you set us up with a bottle of your finest pale ale, and a cup of coffee for my young friend here."

"OK, if you go sit in the back, I will bring them right over."

"Are you going to join us?" John asked.

"Don't mind if I do."

The man and boy found a table, and John took out a pack of cigarettes. Conor spotted a book of matches on the table with "The Preacher" printed in gold letters on it. He tore out a match like he had seen John do many times, struck it against the black strip on the bottom and held it for the man while he lit up the cigarette. He blew out the match and placed it into the ashtray. The boy looked at him and pointing to the packet of cigarettes said, "Those are one of the three things that are damaging your health."

"You are not wrong." He paused, turned his head to look at the ceiling and while blowing out smoke said quietly to himself, "But shut up about it."

Tony arrived with a mug of coffee, a large bottle of beer with a frosted beer mug and a bottle of Coca Cola.

As he sat down at the table, Tony grabbed the Coke bottle and held it out in front of him. They clinked their drinks together as Tony said, "To absent friends."

The boy said, "This is a really nice bar. Why the bar trade?"

SONGS *and* PORTOBELLOS

Tony looked at him. "I tried a lot of things after my spell in the army, but nothing seemed to fit with me. I used to spend a lot of time at this side of the counter, and the guy that owned this place wanted to sell, so I thought to myself why not try the other side of the counter. Then I woke up one morning owning a bar in Greenwich Village. It all seemed to happen very quickly, thanks to a little help from my friends," and he raised his drink to John.

"What did you do in the army?" the boy asked.

"Two years in Korea '51 and '52."

"What was it like?"

Tony looked down at the table and said, "It was a horror show."

The boy could see that the man was uncomfortable with the subject, and said, "I am sorry I did not mean to be nosey."

"No you are OK, any friend of John's is a friend of mine."

"Were you in Greenwich in '61?"

"What? Do you mean when all the protests were going on?"

"Yes," said the boy.

"Damn right, I was. I was working in a tobacco store by day and playing my sax in a club by night. But I still marched with all the brothers and sisters. Stop us singing? I don't fucking think so."

Conor smiled and said, "The good fight, Tony," and raised his coffee mug in salute.

A broad grin spread across Tony's face and he looked at Conor and said, "Good man yourself."

They were quiet for a little bit, and Tony asked, "How old are you, Conor?"

"Fourteen," said the boy.

"I have a daughter your age, Kathy. She lives in Long Island with her mother."

"I get to see her every other weekend. Myself and her mother broke up a few years back."

The boy looked at him and could see that this hurt him and said, "I am sorry to hear that, Tony."

"Oh well, you've got to take whatever life throws at you and roll with it. Do you want another round here?"

John said, "I am OK with this one." Then he paused and said, "Maybe a shot of Old No. 7, though, might breathe some life into me."

"Coming right up, how about yourself young man?"

"No thank you, Tony, I am fine with this."

With that he skipped off to the bar and came back with a large tumbler full of ice and amber liquid, which he placed in front of John. He then went off serving other customers.

The man and boy sat at the table and John sipped his drink.

"What is Old No. 7?" the boy asked.

"It is another name for Jack Daniel's whiskey."

They were silent for a bit. "Do you have any family?" the boy asked.

"Yes," said the man, "I have been married three times. I have a son and a daughter and grandchildren."

The boy frowned at him and said, "Seriously – three times?"

The man laughed and said, "Yes – three times."

He looked at the boy and said, "How about you? You ever been married?" They both laughed out loud.

"No, came close a couple of times though."

They got up, and John went up to the bar reaching for his wallet and was immediately told by Tony, "Your money is no good in here guys."

They both shook hands with the barman, and he said, "See you again men."

The two left the bar and walked out onto the street.

Chapter 17

It was ten o'clock in the morning and Conor was sitting with Melanie having a cup of coffee in the café beside the tube station at Ladbroke Grove. It was pouring with rain, and they both had umbrellas left in the corner. Melanie was wearing a black shiny raincoat with black knee-length boots. Her matching wide-brimmed hat was on the table in front of her. Conor looked at her and noticed that she was tanned from the summer sun, as was he. The summer holidays were nearly over, and this coming Saturday was his turn to make his presentation on New York, with her presentation the following week.

She asked him, "Are you ready for your fifteen minutes on Saturday?"

He replied thoughtfully, "Yes, I think so. And you for next week?"

"Yes, me too."

"OK then, so what's on the agenda for today then, Melanie?"

She replied, "There is not a lot we can do in this weather, unless it is indoors."

He thought for a while and said, "If you like I could show you the Portobello."

"What is the Portobello?" she asked.

"My pub," was his reply.

She smiled broadly at him. "I'd love to see it. I didn't want to bring it up in case you might have changed your mind."

"No, it's just that the weather has been so good and I guess I was waiting for a rainy day. It is only ten minutes up the road, so we shouldn't get too wet."

She said, "Brilliant, Conor, let's drink up and make our way to the Portobello."

"Don't expect too much. I mean I like it, but you might think that it's a dump."

She said, "I doubt that very much," and she put on her hat and tightened the belt on her raincoat.

The boy paid for the coffees, and they both grabbed their umbrellas and headed up towards Kensal Road.

The rain beat down as they made their way up the street, but they were well protected. They passed the Parish Church of Saint Michael and the Tavistock Pub, and crossed over the iron railway bridge. They turned right onto Kensal Road and walked the hundred or so yards to the door of Conor's flat. He opened the door on the ground floor, and they both shook their umbrellas and left them in the bottom of the coat stand in the hallway. She took off her hat and coat and hung them on the coat stand and straightened her hair with her hands. Under her coat she had on a short black skirt with a wine coloured V-neck jumper.

He went ahead, and showed her how to squeeze between the banister and the wall.

She hesitated slightly and he smiled at her and said, "Come on then, skinny."

She followed him, and he opened the door for her. They stood in front of the smoked glass panel with "Portobello" engraved on it. She looked at him and said, "This is it then, Conor." They rounded the panel and stood in the middle of the pub.

The girl put her hands to her face and then stretched out her arms and just said, "FANTASTIC." She was quiet then for a while and just looked all around her with her mouth open.

"It is everything and yet nothing like I expected."

"How do you mean?" he asked.

"It is much prettier, with its beautiful stage and all. You can feel its presence – if you know what I mean. When did you discover it?"

"I was eight," he said.

"Did it look like this?" And she waved her hand around the room.

"No, it was wrecked, so I had a lot of work to do."

"When you were eight?"

"Yes, mostly, but I have added little bits to it since."

"Can we sit on the stage?" she asked.

"Sure, no problem." He brought over the chair and climbed onto the stage. He held out his hand to her and she caught it and pulled herself up onto the chair and then onto the stage. They made their way across to the little table, sat down and looked down on the bar.

They were quiet for a little while, and he asked, "What are you thinking?"

She looked at him and said, "You can feel the history of the place, it is as if the people who were here, are still here – we just can't see them."

He smiled at her and said, "You get it, don't you?"

She smiled back and said, "Yes I do."

Conor had spent a lot of time the evening before thinking of how he could get Melanie to meet John. He could not rationalise why he wanted to do this, was it to impress her, or was it because he wanted her to experience and learn what he had? As he thought about it more, he came to the conclusion that it was something more intuitive than rational and he decided to accept it. He decided he did not want to bring Melanie through the door and out into New York, because he did not know what would happen, and also she might think he was insane. Likewise, bringing John through the door from New York to London was not a good option. It was then that he came up with the idea. He thought, if I bring John through the door but only as far as the stage, and had Melanie enter from Kensal Road and join them, it might work. He came to the conclusion that perhaps the pub was actually the junction between the two places, that it was neither in London nor New York.

As they sat on the stage, he turned to the girl and asked, "Do you remember my friend John?"

"Yes, the writer."

"His health isn't as good as it should be at the moment, but I was thinking about getting you to meet him."

"I would love to," she said.

He continued, "I was thinking about the three of us meeting here. What do you think?"

"What, here in the pub?"

"Yes," he said.

She smiled and said, "Conor, it would be perfect here. Do you think we could bring some wine and maybe some food?"

He smiled at her and said, "Yes, I think that would be very nice. I will chat with John about it and see what he says."

She looked at him and said, "You know, I feel very privileged that you have shared this place with me. Thank you." He smiled at her and said, "You are welcome here anytime, but you cannot tell anyone about it."

She sat back on her chair and just said, "Never."

He looked at her and knew that his secret was completely safe.

She asked him, "So is this where you go when you want to write or study."

"Yes, it is my place. I find that I can think more clearly here than anywhere else. Where do you go to think?" he asked her.

"In Brighton we had a roof garden, and I used to go up there when I wanted to think. It was always private, apart from the seagulls that made an enormous racket."

"Do you have somewhere in London?"

"Not yet, I will find somewhere, I am sure. But right now I will have to make do with my bedroom?"

Conor looked around the pub and said, "I would be lost without this place."

She looked at him and smiled saying, "Yes, I can see that, Conor."

They chatted on for a long while, and then they got up from the table and made their way off the stage and out of the pub into the hallway. She put on her coat and hat, and picked up her umbrella. She said, "I will see you tomorrow then at ten o'clock in the usual place."

"Hold on" he said, "let me walk you down to the tube station."

"Not just a hero, but also a gentleman," she said with a grin.

"The full package," he said.

Later that same day, Conor and the writer sat in their usual spot in Washington Square. He looked at the man, and thought he was looking more and more tired, but he also knew it was pointless asking him about it. While the morning had been pouring with rain in London, the morning in New York was baking hot. The boy thought to himself: another complication. They had been discussing John's amazing life. He painted pictures with his words about beautiful places and adventures that he had, and the people he had met. The man was so knowledgeable that it was just a joy to listen to him. The boy's summer had been filled with these wonderful stories and he sat enraptured.

They were silent for a little while, then the boy turned to the man and said, "I have a friend that I would like you to meet."

"Who is it?" asked the man.

"She is my friend from school."

"Is she over from London?"

The boy paused and said, "Yes, she lives in London."

The man grinned and said, "Oh, I see this is the girlfriend, then. Why do you want me to meet her?"

"She is one of the brightest people I have ever met, and she wants to be a journalist."

"I don't expect that she is pretty at all?"

Without thinking about the question, Conor said immediately, "Oh God, yes."

They both laughed.

"OK, so when is this grand introduction to take place?" said John.

"I was hoping tomorrow, if it is OK for you?"

"Where? At The Preacher?"

The boy said, "I was thinking about somewhere else that is a little different."

"Like where?" said the man.

"OK, there is an old bar under the flat where I am staying that has been closed down for a few years. It is really nice and even has a little stage. It is somewhere that I discovered and I use it to sit and think. I thought we could bring a little food and maybe some wine and have a chat."

John smiled and said, "It sounds like a grand idea. Is it far from here?"

The boy said, "It is just down off Bleecker Street, but there is only one thing that I ask of you," said the boy.

"What's that then?" Said the man.

"When you enter the place leave your preconceived ideas at the door."

The man laughed out loud remembering the trip to the Guggenheim and said, "Sounds like a fun trip. Right now I fancy some ice cream. How about you?"

"Yes, sure," said the boy.

They got up and made their way through the Waverly Place entrance and towards Baldini's Ice Cream Emporium.

As they walked John said, "You know you and this girl."

"Yes," said the boy.

"I reckon you have it bad."

The boy smiled a little smile to himself at the comment, and stuck his hands into the pockets of his jeans as they walked together towards Baldini's.

Chapter 18

The following morning the two youngsters met at Ladbroke Grove station and were now in the convenience shop at the corner of Westbourne Park Road. It was a quarter past ten, and Conor had told the girl about the planned meeting with John for later that day. He had figured that if he got John to the Portobello before Melanie arrived, she would not see them enter from under the stage. His plan was to get John there for a quarter past four and Melanie at half past. He hated the idea of being deceptive to either John or the girl, but he just did not know how to explain the situation to them. Allowing for the time difference in New York, he had told John that he would meet him at eleven in Washington Square. Conor knew that leaving the pub was also going to be a problem, but he decided to himself that he would sort that out later.

He had thought long and hard about how the conversation between Melanie and John might go. Will he ask her about how she likes New York, or will she ask him how he likes London? He smiled to himself when he thought of the absurdity of the situation. He eventually figured to hell with it, let whatever happens, happen. It would be easier for them to find out about the door in that way, than him trying to explain it to either of them alone. When he reached this conclusion he was quite pleased that he had managed to rationalise an irrational situation.

In the shop, and after much debate, Conor carried a basket which held a long French loaf, two wedges of cheddar cheese and two bottles of French red wine. The selection of the wine had been tricky, as neither youngster new anything much about wine. They had settled on a wine that had a label on it with a small gold star proclaiming that it was a Bordeaux champion vineyard 1963. They thought that with the gold star it looked better than the rest, and anyway the choice was limited to two reds and two whites.

The shop smelled of cooked ham, washing powder and newspapers. The man behind the counter wore a brown shop coat with what looked like about twenty pens and pencils in the top pocket. He had a fat red face and a yard brush of a moustache. As they approached the counter he spoke sharply in a strong cockney accent, "Hang on a minute – I can't sell you wine, you're not old enough." The girl looked at him with a kind of shocked expression and suddenly burst out laughing "Of course not. You thought these are for us," and she laughed again pointing to the bottles. "These are for a lunch we are giving for a friend who is probably older than yourself."

She spoke with such confidence that all the man said was, "All right then, just so long as they are not for you."

Conor smiled to himself.

The shopkeeper went to the till and rang up the different items. He looked at the two and said, "That will be four pounds, two shillings and sixpence when you are ready."

They had pooled their resources beforehand, and had a total of five pounds, ten shillings and three pence between them. Melanie had charge of the money and she counted out the correct amount onto the counter. The shopkeeper placed the coins and notes into different compartments in the till and closed it shut.

They gathered the wine with the bread and cheese and put them into a paper carrier bag that the man had handed them. Conor took the bag, and as they were going through the shop the girl stopped and asked, "Do you have any candle stick holders at home?"

He thought for a little while and remembered the two brass candlesticks that his mother kept in a cupboard in the kitchen, "Yes, we have two."

She said OK and went back to the counter, "Can I have two white candles as well please?"

The man reached behind him into a drawer and held out three candles of different lengths, "What size do you want, love?"

The girl looked at them carefully and picked out the middle size. The shopkeeper pulled down a sheet of brown paper that was on a roller fixed to the wall behind him. By pulling the paper upwards against a flat metal plate, that was part of the roller, it cut neatly from the roll. He placed the square of brown paper onto the counter and set down the two candles in the corner. He then rolled the candles and paper tightly until he had a long flat tube. Taking a piece of Sellotape from the dispenser on the counter, he secured the brown paper tube. Folding each end inwards he taped these also so it was a neat parcel.

"That will be sixpence love – thrupence each."

The girl handed him the money and said, "Thank you."

"You are welcome, luv, see you again," said the man.

She took the package and joined the boy who was waiting at the door.

As they walked, they passed the small public garden in Westbourne Park, and she beckoned him to sit on a bench under a big horse chestnut tree. She counted out the money she had left over and gave the boy his share. They sat in silence with their shopping between them.

He could see that she was thinking for a while and then she said, "I think the easiest option is if I bring home the bread and cheese, and set it out on some paper plates along with some other bits and pieces. I have some plastic knives and forks back at the house. What do you think, Conor?"

"Sounds great, if you don't mind doing it," said the boy.

He reached into his pocket and brought out a key and said, "You can let yourself in the front door, it is number 248, and you know how to get into the pub from there."

She sat upright and asked, "Is John going to be able to get past the stairs? It is a bit of a tight squeeze even for me."

Conor smiled and said, "It is OK. There is another door that I have a key for."

She smiled and said, "OK, now let's think of what else we need."

She thought for a little while and asked, "Do you have some wine glasses, and, oh yes, a corkscrew?"

"Yes, no problem, I will bring them down along with the pair of candle sticks from our flat upstairs."

She looked at him with a smile and said, "I am really looking forward to this."

"Me too," said the boy.

She took the bread and cheese and placed them into her shoulder bag, and handed him back the shopping bag with the bottles of wine and candles. She looked at him sideways and asked,

"Are you going to be drinking wine?"

"I don't know – maybe."

She smiled and said, "I will bring a flask of tea, with some paper cups."

He looked at her and said, "You think of everything, don't you?"

They sat together for a while without speaking.

Then she turned to him and asked, "When did you first meet John?"

"It was early this summer when I just bumped into him. He was sitting on a park bench and we just got to talking."

He paused for a while and said, "I don't know how to describe it but we just seemed to hit it off straight away."

The boy laughed and said, "I asked him what he does, and he told me he was a writer. I asked him if he was a good writer."

The girl laughed and said, "That is so typical of you. What did he say?"

Conor did his best to copy John's American accent and said in a gravelly voice, "What a fucking question!"

The girl laughed out loud.

The boy looked at her and said, "I have found him to be an inspiration, but I am worried about his health."

"Why so?" she asked.

"As the summer has gone by, he just seems to look more tired and drawn."

She sat quietly for a little while, and then she looked at him and said, "I am going to miss this summer when we go back to school. It has been wonderful."

"Yes," he said, "like no other summer."

She said, "I have learned so much just travelling around, and not just about London."

"In what sense?"

"Well, I suppose I have come to know you, and you can be wise in your own way."

"But an enigma."

She put her hands to her head and said, "Oh God, I knew I

should never have said that. I was just searching for something clever to say."

"Well, when you find it, will you let me know?"

"OK, Conor, you will be the first to know," she said with a smile on her face.

Eventually she got up and said, "OK then, let's get sorted out for this afternoon when I get to meet your friend, John."

They strolled the short distance to the garden entrance.

She looked at him and said, "Right then, half past four," and she turned left towards Westbourne Park.

As she left he watched her walk away. She had a grace and elegance that made her stand out from the crowd. He could only describe it as a presence and it radiated all around her.

She called back to him, "See you later."

"OK then," he said.

Chapter 19

The boy had spent the later part of the morning and afternoon tidying the pub. He had always managed to keep it neat and tidy, but he put in a special effort today. He swept the stage and the floor, and with some furniture polish he had managed to get a shine on the bar and the bits of the piano and tables that weren't damaged. He had a little bottle of brass cleaner, and with a cloth, he applied this to the beer pumps and foot rail at the bar. He had seen his mother do this before with the brass ornaments upstairs in the flat. The liquid is left to dry a little, and in the process it turns a chalky white. It is then rubbed off with gusto leaving the brass behind glittering. When he looked back from the stage the brass sparkled.

He had borrowed a red checked tablecloth from upstairs along with the two brass candle sticks. He sat on the stage in the chair, and with one of the candle sticks on his lap he applied the brass polish to it and placed it on the table. He repeated this with the second candle stick and sat and watched them turn white. He took each one in turn, and he rubbed off the brass polish vigorously until they shone like the bar taps. He took the two white candles that he had stuck in his top pocket, and placing the candle sticks on the floor of the stage he pressed the candles firmly into place. He was very careful to make sure that the candles were straight, and he thought to himself with a smile, this is something that his old friend Tom the caretaker would do very well.

He set the tablecloth on to the table, and in the centre he placed the two candles in their holders. He looked around and thought it would be nice to have one of the candles in front of the mirror behind the bar. With that, he jumped off the stage and placed the candle stick on one of the glass shelves in front of the mirror. He jumped back onto the stage, reached down and picked up the paper shopping bag off the floor. One of the wine bottles and three wine glasses were set out on the table along with a corkscrew and a white tea towel. The glasses were rubbed with the tea towel until they shone and he even polished the bottle of wine. He thought to himself that he should open the wine. His father and mother had wine on special occasions, and he had observed the opening of a bottle of wine many times before. This last Christmas his father had showed him the process step by step, so he was not at all daunted by the task. He placed the tip of the corkscrew under the red seal that covered the cork at top of the bottle. He used the sharp tip of the corkscrew to pick at the seal until he had caused it to split. With his finger, he peeled off the seal and removed it completely. He placed the corkscrew tip close to the centre of the cork and screwed it in until all of the screw disappeared in to the cork. Placing the bottle between his knees, and with a sharp tug, he pulled the cork with a loud pop. He cleaned the neck of the bottle with the tea towel, and placed the bottle on the table. Taking the cork, he pushed it back a little into the bottle. He had turned the cork around so that the side of the cork that was red from the wine was pointing outward.

He sat back, reviewed the scene and was satisfied with his handy work. Sitting here in this place with Melanie and John was going to be a very special moment for him. He thought: I will light the candles to see how it all looks. But, with what? He jumped off the stage and ran upstairs to the flat. He fumbled in the top pocket of his jacket for the key and pulled out the book of matches with "The Preacher" printed on it in gold letters. He smiled to himself, walked downstairs and made his way back into the pub and up onto the stage. Before he climbed onto the stage, he picked up an ashtray from one of the tables, and placed it onto the table alongside the candle. He took out a match, struck it and lit the candle. He jumped off the stage, lit the candle behind the bar and climbed onto the bar counter to sit down and look at the stage.

What was in front of him was like a scene from a play. The light from the candle cast a shadow of the wine bottle and glasses onto the wall of the log cabin. The entire stage seemed to come to life and the place felt warm and welcoming. For ten minutes he alternated between sitting on the stage and sitting on the bar. He suddenly thought: God, what is the time? Looking at his watch he saw it was a quarter to four. With that, he jumped off the counter and ran up to the flat. Rapidly he changed his clothes to the denim jacket, beige jeans and navy sweater combination. He washed his face and hands, and without much success ran a brush through his hair. Gathering himself he said, "OK, here we go." As he went through the stage he thought he would leave the candles lighting as they were well secured in the candlesticks, and at five minutes to eleven o'clock, New York time, he was walking up Bleecker Street towards Washington Square.

He found John sitting on the bench at the usual spot in the square. The boy waved as he walked towards him and said, "Hi, how are you? Are you ready?"

"Sure am," said the man.

They walked out of the square and down Thompson Street. After one hundred yards or so, they turned right onto Bleecker Street. It was a warm August day but there was a gentle breeze blowing that was keeping the temperature down. They were moving slowly because John was stiffer and more laboured than usual.

"Are you OK?" The boy asked.

"It is like I told you – fucked," John said with a grin.

"Will you make it through lunch?" the boy said mischievously.

John stopped, looked at the boy and said, "Fuck knows." They both laughed.

Soon they reached the blue concrete steps and the door.

Conor gestured to the man, "Here we are."

"What? Down there?"

"Yes, this is it. It is much nicer inside," said the boy.

"You would hope," John said a little apprehensively.

Conor skipped down the steps and beckoned John to follow. When the two stepped inside, Conor locked the door behind them and guided the man up the steps and onto the stage. He turned and pulled the door back down onto the stage and went over to the table.

John looked all around him, "What magic is here," and he looked at the boy with a sparkle in his eye that the boy had not seen for a while.

Stretching out his arms he turned to face the bar and said in a booming voice, "All the world's a stage."

Conor held a chair for him that had its back to the door under the stage, and the man sat down. He then pulled the cork from the wine bottle and poured the man a glass of wine. He took another glass and poured a little for himself and sat down at the table.

They clinked glasses and Conor said, "Welcome to the Portobello. What do you think of it, John?"

The man looked at the boy with a smile and then slowly looked around him and back to the boy. "Conor, this is where dreams are made."

The boy smiled at him and said, "I knew you would like it."

The man looked around again and said, "So, this is somewhere that you spend a lot of your time."

"Yes, this place helps me to think." He waved his arm around him, "When I come in here I feel like I am somewhere else – I am not sure where."

"How do you mean?" the man asked.

"When I sit here the thoughts flow around in my head. It might sound odd, but here is where the weight that I carry in my head is removed. I feel I have no restrictions, and my thoughts become crystal clear."

John was smiling at him, "Not odd at all, Conor. Is your friend coming?"

"Yes, she will be here shortly."

"Do you not want to open the door for her?" And he pointed down to the door on the stage floor.

"Oh no, she will come in the other entrance," and he pointed to the smoked-glass partition to the right of them.

As they sipped their wine, John took out a cigarette, leaned forward and lit it from the candle.

He blew smoke into the air and asked, "So tell me, then, what do you think of New York?"

The boy thought for a while and said, "I find it is a place that rewards success and punishes failure, and there is no pity for failure and none expected."

"Are you saying it has no compassion?"

The boy looked down onto the stage, thought for a while and

then looked at the man and said, "In some ways yes, but I see it as honest, and that makes it beautiful and unique."

"Where do you think this honesty comes from?" asked the man.

The boy smiled and said, "From the people that have come to New York down the centuries. They probably have come from places where they were at the bottom of the social pile but had the courage to take the chance."

The man said, "But New York is a cold society."

Conor looked at him and said, "Yes, but a fair one."

They sat in silence for a little while as John blew smoke from his cigarette into the air the boy topped up the man's glass. Conor drank very little of his own wine because he did not much care for the taste, but he thought it would be impolite to have the man drink on his own.

As Conor was pouring the wine, John caught sight of the label and said, "A Bordeaux no less."

When he had sat back down, he looked at the boy and said, "Do you see a lot of difference between New York and London?"

"Yes I do."

"How so?"

"In London, position in society seems to be the goal, whereas in New York money seems to be the goal."

The man smiled to himself and asked, "Which do you think is the more just?"

"I think neither. There must be a better way to exist."

The man took another swallow of his wine and turning to the boy said, "Conor you have a unique perspective. Don't ever let assholes, no matter who they think they are, tell you what is right and what is wrong or how you should think. Make me a promise right here and right now that you will fight anyone that tries to change you."

Conor reached across the table and held out his hand, "I promise." They shook hands firmly and John took another sip of wine.

They turned towards the partition as they heard the sound of someone entering the pub.

Chapter 20

Melanie came into view carrying a canvas shoulder bag. She had on a beige raincoat over a deep blue dress with a wide-brimmed, black hat complete with a blue silk ribbon that reached down her back nearly to her waist. Conor thought she looked stunning and he went over and helped her onto the chair and then onto the stage. She strode across to John with her arm outstretched and John rose from his chair and took her hand.

"I am very pleased to meet you," she said, "I am Melanie."

"The pleasure is mine. I am John."

She smiled broadly and said, "I have brought a few snacks and some tea. I will put them out." She first took off her coat and placed it on the back of her chair, and set her hat down on the dresser. Placing the bag on her chair, she took out three dishes covered in foil and put them onto the table. She then set out paper side plates, napkins, knives, forks and spoons for the three of them. She uncovered the dishes to reveal sliced cheese and bread with butter, various kinds of salad and a small bowl with a savoury dip. Finally she took out a thermos flask with some cups and saucers and a little container for milk and sugar. She did all of this with no effort, and it seemed to be all done in a matter of seconds.

John looked at the table and said, "This looks wonderful."

She smiled at him and said, "Please, help yourself."

The girl poured tea for herself and they started eating the food.

As they were eating John said, "Conor tells me that you are at school together."

She smiled at the boy and then turned to the man and said, "Yes – St Charles. I have not been there too long as we moved from Brighton earlier this year."

"So London is your home now?"

"Yes."

"So what do you think of London?"

"I love it – it is so full of life and energy. And what do you think of Conor's pub, the Portobello?" she asked.

"Wonderful, I don't think I have ever had lunch on a stage before."

Conor topped up John's glass, and then asked the girl for a cup of tea. She poured it out and winked at him. John sat back on the chair and wiped his mouth with a napkin. "Good wine, good food and good company. Thank you, both." The two youngsters smiled at each other and then at the man.

John looked around him and said without looking at either the boy or girl, "I wonder who else strode this stage. Magicians, actors, chancers and clowns – who knows?" He continued, "Shakespeare wrote, 'All the world's a stage and all the men and women merely players; they have their exits and their entrances and one man in his time plays many parts.'"

She looked at him smiled and said, "*As You Like It*. I always found it fascinating that he said: all the men and women merely players and one man in his time plays many parts".

The man smiled to himself, and then looked at both of them in turn as he lit a cigarette.

John then said to the girl, "Do you like Shakespeare?"

"Yes, very much. We used to travel up to London to see whichever play was running at the time in the West End."

"So which play is your favourite?" the man asked.

Her face became a little serious as she thought, and then she looked up at him and said, "I have not seen all the plays, but of the ones I have seen, I would say all of *Hamlet* and *Romeo and Juliet* up to the beginning of act three."

John looked at her quizzically and asked, "Why not all of *Romeo and Juliet?*"

"At the beginning of act three Mercutio dies, and curses both their houses. I think he also puts a curse on the play from there."

John smiled to himself and said, as he lifted his wine glass, "Have you had any tutorials or lectures on Shakespeare."

"No," said the girl, "I have only seen the plays."

"That is wonderful," he said. "I am going to say to you what I have been telling my friend Conor here all summer. Don't ever let your education dictate to you how you should perceive and interpret. Your perception is unique."

Conor topped up the man's wine glass.

"I have not seen you so quiet since I first met you, Conor," said the man.

"It is funny, but this is the place where I go to think on my own, so I suppose I am in the habit of being quiet in here."

The man looked around and said, "I will carry the image of this place with me always."

John then looked at the girl and said, "Conor tells me you want to be a journalist."

She smiled, "Yes, it is something that I have wanted since I was very small."

"Why? What is it about journalism specifically?"

Melanie sat back in her chair, and said, "My father took me to the offices of the local paper in Brighton when I was eight. He is a commercial artist, and he was doing some work for them. I was sitting in the reception when a lady came in. She introduced herself as Sandra and asked who I was. I told her my name, and she said for me to come along with her and she would give me a tour of the place. She took me into the printing room and commercial desks and explained the process of making the weekly publication. When we went into the newsroom she went into her office and it had 'Editor' in golden letters on the glass door."

The girl continued, "I asked her what her job was, and she said that she was the editor, and she was responsible for the commercial success of the paper. She also said that it was her responsibility to ensure that the news published was fair and honest, irrespective of what or whom the article or piece was about. She described to me the fine line between writing the truth, and sensationalising or biasing the truth. We struck up an immediate friendship, and from then on I used to call to see her whenever I could. She always gave me her time and was a very big influence on me."

The girl grew a little quiet and said, "She died in a car accident in 1964." She looked at them both with very sad eyes and said, "I kept the beautiful piece that they wrote about her in the paper." She paused a little and said, "I knew straight away that I wanted to be like her, and as I got a little older, I started to think more about what she had told me about the truth." She looked straight at John and said, "I see media as having a very powerful influence on society, and journalism is therefore a potent weapon. I re-read many times all of the beautiful things that they said about her after she died. I often wondered if she would have agreed with the content, and if she didn't, would she have made them change it. I am certain that if there was anything sentimental or irrelevant in describing her or her life, she would have them take it out."

John looked at her warmly and said, "I believe that when you lose someone that is close to you, you take the things that you admire about them, like courage and character, and put them with your own. That way, the spirit that sets them apart, lives on within you." He pointed to the girl and said, "She lives on within you."

She looked at him and smiled, "What is it like being a writer?"

He looked at them both and said, "Sometimes it is simple and other times it can be very difficult. As a writer of novels I often have to embed my message in allegory.

I expect you both know this, but allegory in writing is delivering a notion or idea indirectly through the narrative. For example in Hemmingway's novel *The Old Man and the Sea*, he writes about an old man's battle to catch a big fish, but his allegory is the man's heroic struggle with his age and his changing identity. One of the most evil things in this world is nothingness. In some ways the old man's struggle is with nothingness. Do you see?"

The boy and girl both said, "Yes" together.

"My whole career has been spent avoiding being opinionated in my work, which sometimes I have failed at by the way."

Conor said, "That sounds very difficult."

"It can be frustrating. I call it the dance."

They sat for a little time while John smoked and Conor topped up the man's glass with the last of the bottle of wine. Eventually he said, "You know, I see in you both great promise."

They looked at each other and smiled.

"Stop smirking," he said. He then looked at the girl and said, "You know very clearly what you want to do and you are going to be a force of nature young lady." He turned to the boy and said, "Conor, you are a pilgrim soul and will find your path – you have a gift."

Melanie looked at the man and asked, "Have you ever been in love?"

"There are many kinds of love, which do you mean?"

"Like poetic love."

The writer was silent, and then said, "No, I have been married three times and have loved them all, but never felt poetic love."

"Do you think it exists?"

"In the vastness of the universe, I believe everything exists."

She smiled at him and asked, "Is it worth seeking?"

"If there is the tiniest chance of merging your soul with another's, then I believe it is truly heroic and should be pursued."

There was a connection between the three of them that seemed to make everything outside of a small circle around the table go out of focus. Not once did they mention London or New York, and it seemed like they were suspended between the two places. They talked on for a while, but Conor looked across at John and could see that he was visibly tiring.

"Are you OK, John?"

The man said, "I am OK."

Conor looked at Melanie and without any prompt she said, "I am going to have to head away."

John smiled at her and he understood the connection between the two – their unspoken words.

SONGS *and* PORTOBELLOS

She emptied the remains of the food into a plastic bag that she had brought and poured the remains of the tea from cups back into the thermos. In just a short number of movements, everything except the wine glasses and the empty wine bottle were left on the table, the rest was in her canvas shoulder bag. She looked at Conor, smiled and said, "I will see you tomorrow at ten."

"OK, see you then."

She got up, gathered her hat and coat, went over to John and bent down and kissed him on the cheek, "Thank you so much John, I am delighted to have met you."

John looked at her and said, "You are going to put the fear of God into a lot of people in time to come, I am certain of it."

She smiled at him, strode off the stage and disappeared behind the smoked glass panel and out of the bar.

The writer looked at Conor and just said, "Seeing young people like her gives me such hope. She is, without doubt, already a force of nature."

Conor smiled at the man.

They both got up, and the boy opened the door on the stage and they went out onto Bleecker Street. Conor locked the door behind them.

John stopped up and said, "I can't remember having a better time, but shit it was cold in there." Then they walked off towards Washington Square.

Chapter 21

Conor walked John as far as The Preacher, and said goodbye to him there. The boy strolled back towards the pub feeling a rich sense of satisfaction about how it had all gone. There was something magical about the afternoon that he couldn't describe. He entered through the door at 248 and went up onto the stage locking the door behind him. The candles still burned, and when he looked across to the bar, he had never seen it look better. He took his time tidying up the Portobello, and gathered the wine glasses to bring them upstairs along with the corkscrew and table cloth. He blew out both candles and gathered the candle sticks. He took one of the candles and pressed it firmly into the empty wine bottle, and left it along with the other candle and second full bottle of wine on the table.

Upstairs in the flat, he washed and dried the glasses and put them away with the other bits and pieces. As he went into the kitchen he turned on the radio. When it had warmed up he tuned it to Radio Luxembourg and went to make a cup of coffee. He boiled the kettle and took out the jar of Maxwell House and made himself a cup. Radio Luxembourg usually faded in and out, but it was crystal clear this evening. The DJ played 'Ruby Tuesday' and then 'A Whiter Shade of Pale'. The boy sat at the table sipping his coffee and listening to the music: "We skipped the light fandango, turned cartwheels cross the floor." He did not know what the song was about, but it had what he could only describe as a beautiful mood to it. Just as the song was ending, he could hear the key turn in the front door, and in stepped his parents laden down with shopping bags. He had not seen them for quite some time, and during the course of this particular summer, this arrangement had suited him very well.

His mother took the shopping bags into the kitchen, turned down the radio and started putting away the groceries into the cupboards. The boy got up and went over to the sink to wash out his cup. She looked at the boy and said, "I'd swear that you have gotten taller. It has been that long since we've seen you. It's like having a ghost around the place; you know it's there but you can't see it."

The boy smiled and said, "It has been a great summer."

"Great in what way? What have you been up to?"

"Oh, just the school project has kept me very busy, and I have met some really nice new friends." He said this with a real happiness in his voice.

His mother stopped putting away the groceries and looked at him more closely. She turned around and called out, "Pat, come in here. You'd better tell him."

"Tell him what?" asked the boy.

His father came into the kitchen. "Sit down, Conor, we have some great news to tell you. You know how we have both been working a lot over the summer, and we did not take our holiday this year?"

"Yes," said the boy with a growing sense of apprehension.

"Well, we have been saving to go to Ireland."

"But we can't go to Ireland – school starts in a weeks' time."

The father put his hand on the boy's shoulder, "We are not going for a holiday this time, we are going back home to live."

The boy felt a numbness coming over him and he sat there without speaking.

"When we found out about your summer school project we did not want to tell you as it would have distracted you. So, Conor, what do you say to that?"

For a while the boy could say nothing at all, and eventually he turned to his mother and just asked, "When?"

"We go this Sunday week," she said, but she wasn't smiling like the father, as she sensed the boy was not happy with the news.

"In one weeks' time," was all the boy said and just looked off into space.

His father said, "The plan is we are going to stay with your Aunt Leena in Kildare for a few months until we get a place of our own. I have a job got with the Electricity Supply Board in Dublin, so we are all sorted out."

The mother added, "They have a great school in Kildare run by the Brothers, and you will make friends there in no time."

The boy could not speak.

His father said, "It will be good for us all to be back home again. London is great to earn money, but you can't beat being home."

The boy just looked at him, without speaking.

His mother began to see more clearly that he was very upset by the news, and changed the subject by saying, "I'll make a pot of tea – I have some pastries that I got when I was in town."

The father said, "Right so, here is the plan. Next week you will need to get your clothes and books sorted. There is a removals van coming next Saturday, so I will need you to help me to get it loaded up. The smaller bits and pieces that we have left over, we can bring in the car on Sunday." He got up and slapped the boy on the shoulder and said, "It will be the makings of you – wait and see."

The boy turned to his mother and said, "I don't think I will bother with the tea. I might just go out for a walk, if that is OK?"

She looked at him and said, "Go on then, off with you. But get back early, I don't want you out all hours."

As the boy got up, his father reached into his pocket and pulled out a red, ten-shilling note and pressed it into the boy's hand.

The boy looked at it and said nothing.

"Buy yourself something nice to bring home."

The boy looked at him again, unable to say anything.

"And for Christ's sake get a haircut! You are not going home looking like that."

The boy just quietly said, "Thanks," and left the flat with the ten-shilling note tightly pressed in his hand.

Conor walked up Kensal Road to where it intersected with Ladbroke Grove, and stood on the corner. His head was throbbing, and his summer flashed before him in a blizzard of images. He walked across the big old metal railway bridge and the familiar squeal of the train wheels against the tracks below sounded louder than normal. It was a very still August evening and the light was beginning to fade. As he crossed the bridge, there was a pungent smell in the air that he often got in tube stations. He felt that his world was crumbling around him, and everything that he had found during this summer was suddenly being taken away.

Down the road he could see the lights of the Tavistock Pub and the revellers drinking their pints of beer out on the footpath.

SONGS *and* PORTOBELLOS

As he walked, the sound of the train wheels was replaced with loud voices, laughter and breaking glass. The pungent smell of the trains changed to beer, cigarettes and chips. He turned down off Ladbroke Grove to the quietness of St Charles Square, and slowly made his way down towards the gates of the school. There was a small green area with a bench, and he turned towards it and sat down heavily. He leaned forward and placed his head in his hands. It was all gone – Melanie, John, school – and was going to be replaced with what, he did not know.

He sat in silence for a while as the darkness started to descend. The street lamps came on very dimly, but they got brighter as they warmed up. The people in the houses in front of him were sitting in their living rooms and he could see the flickering light from television sets reflected in their faces. The boy felt very much alone as he struggled to come to terms with what was happening to him.

A small white dog came wandering up the road and came over to investigate the boy. He sniffed at the boys shoes for a long time and the boy thought that maybe he smelled New York from them. After his curiosity was satisfied, the dog continued up the road in no particular hurry. Conor turned to look at the walls of St Charles school, and he thought of all the times he had spent here. He thought of old Tom and Miss Martin, but mostly he thought of Melanie. It was only a few months now since he had first met her, but it seemed like he had known her all of his life.

He put his head in his hands and thought of John and the wonderful times that they spent together in New York. He did not know what lay ahead of him in Ireland, but he felt he was losing the magic from his life. Tomorrow was Saturday and it was Miss Martin's class. He was in the first group of presentations and all that he could think of right now, was just how pointless it all was. His head was throbbing and he could feel the anger rise from deep within him and he released it with a loud roar, "FUCK, FUCK, FUCK." It seemed to go on for an age and echoed around the darkening empty streets. Then he sat back on the bench and just stared up at the dark grey sky.

Part 3

Chapter 22

It was Saturday morning and Conor was due in Miss Martin's class at ten o'clock. He had slept very little, and he hated the idea of facing the class. Melanie had been on his mind all night long, and he had come to the realisation that the thoughts of not seeing her hurt him the most. He wandered around the flat, made himself a coffee, and eventually got himself ready for school. There was a bundle of papers on his bedside table on his project which included his essay on New York and his presentation notes. He placed them all into the leather satchel that he kept hanging on the chair in his bedroom. At ten minutes to ten, he went to the door and then slowly out of the flat with his satchel under his arm.

The weight of the world was on his shoulders as he walked down Kensal Road. Feelings of anger and frustration bubbled up in him. He had a sensation in his stomach that felt like an emptiness from hunger. As he turned down towards the school, he could see Melanie waiting for him at the gate. Even from where he was at the end of the road, he could see her broad smile and he thought to himself, above anything else I hate the thoughts of making her unhappy.

As he came closer he could barely look at her.

"I had a fantastic time yesterday. I couldn't sleep last night," she said.

"Neither could I," he said.

She saw the troubled look on his face and her expression changed to one of concern, "What's wrong, Conor?"

"We are moving to Ireland."

She stared at him for a little while and then said, "When?"

"Next Sunday."

Her lips tightened and he could sense her anger. She shouted at him, "So when did you decide to tell me?"

He said softly to her, "Melanie, I only found out last night."

It was clear that she was not listening to him as she said, "Of all the horrible things to do, this is the worst. I thought you were my friend."

Again he said softly, "Melanie, I only found out last night."

But again she was not listening, "I trusted you and you, you do this and not let me know. I am never going to speak to you again – ever." And with that she turned her back to him.

For the first time he saw the little girl in her, petulant and difficult. As he looked at her back he said, "Melanie, I only found out last night."

She said nothing but just kept her back turned towards him. He walked around her to face her, but she just turned away, keeping her back to him. He tried to face her again, but she did the same thing keeping her face away from him.

He caught her by the arms and turned her around. Tears were in her eyes and he felt unbelievably sad. He just put his arms around her and held her to him. After a little while she got out her hanky and dried her face, carefully wiping away her tears. They stood in silence for a while just looking at each other.

She said, "I am so sorry. I know it is not your fault, but

during this summer you have become a part of my life and you leaving makes me feel like I am losing a part of me. Does that make any sense?"

He said, "It makes no sense at all, but it is exactly how I feel too. Do we have to go to this class today?"

She looked at him and said, "Yes we do. You are making your presentation and I want to hear it."

He realised that he had no choice in the matter, and just said, "OK," and they turned towards the school and headed for the classroom.

The two youngsters sat beside each other in the classroom. They did not normally do this, but they did so on this Saturday. Miss Martin came in and said, "Well, I am delighted to see you all here. Today half of you are going to give a presentation of your project and the other half next Saturday. Now remember what the project was." She paused and said, "It was to write an essay on your visit to the city you chose, and give a fifteen-minute presentation to the class that expresses your own opinion of the city's culture and society. As you come up to give your presentation, place your essays here," and she pointed to a shelf that was labelled, "The city library". "In the course of the year you can read up on each other's exploits. Today though is all about your fifteen minutes."

She said, "This Saturday we are going through five cities: Paris, Rome, Berlin, Madrid and New York," and she wrote them in order on the blackboard. "OK so, Paris, you are first on stage. I will time you and let you know when your time is up. And don't worry if you run out of things to say, you can always sing a song." The look of horror from the youngsters told her that singing was not an option. A nervous-looking girl called

Irene made her way to the top of the class with a bundle of notes under her arm.

The boy and girl found themselves absorbed in what each of their classmates had to say. Each one had taken on the spirit of the project and tried to provide their own unique insights. At the end of each presentation, Miss Martin started a round of applause and her comments were, "Brilliant job, excellent, fantastic," and as each student sat down, they had a wide grin that showed they were relieved it was over, but that they had thoroughly enjoyed the experience. It was clear that Miss Martin was delighted, and her enthusiasm reached out and was shared by the students.

At last the teacher said, "OK, Conor, you are up, so let's hear about New York." He walked to the front of the room and placed his essay on the shelf. As he looked down at the class he lay down his presentation notes and instead just spoke off the cuff.

"When you look at New York you will see that it is made up of five boroughs or districts – the Bronx, Brooklyn, Manhattan, Queens and Staten Island – and has seven and a half million inhabitants. My focus is going to be on a small part of the Island of Manhattan. Manhattan stretches from Inwood Hill Park in the north down to Battery Park in the south, and is approximately ten miles long and about two miles wide. Distributed throughout the Island are communities from different ethnic backgrounds. Some of these communities are very poor, and some are very wealthy, but they generally coexist very well. When you look deeper at Manhattan you will find a small community to the south of the Island, which is called Greenwich Village. I chose this area of New York for my own insight into the culture and society of the city."

He paused for a while and asked, "Why Greenwich Village?

Greenwich is different from the rest of New York. It is multicultural and its residents are historically more progressive and artistic than the others. If Wall Street is the commercial centre and therefore the financial heartbeat of the city, then Greenwich could be considered New York's soul. Every city has a heartbeat called commerce, but not every city has a soul. Greenwich has had a big impact on culture and society, and not just in New York, but all over the world."

He paused for a little while and then continued, "The Village came to prominence in the late forties and fifties with the rise of the Beat Generation. These were a post-war movement that espoused alternatives to previously held conformist views on art and culture. They were led by poets and writers like Jack Kerouac and Alan Ginsberg, who, with their alternative lifestyles, became the icons of the Beat Generation."

He paused again and saw that he had their attention. "Greenwich was the nucleus of the Beat movement, and the community expressed themselves with abstract and modern art, poetry and music. As time moved on though, the movement became a concern to the city authorities as they saw Greenwich as a threat to law and order. In a more fundamental way, it was a contradiction of their own notions of morality."

The boy sat up onto the desk and sitting on his hands he continued, "The city authorities wanted to eradicate what they believed was a threat to the city, but could they not find socially acceptable ways to do it. What they decided to do was to focus on small practices and make them illegal, thereby bringing down the movement little by little. It was in 1961 that they dreamed up a campaign to ban the singing of songs in Washington Square on Sundays. Washington Square was, and still is, a beautiful little park in the centre of the community – and the focal point for gatherings."

He shrugged his shoulders as he looked around the class, "What did the Greenwich community do? They continued to sing and play their music everyday including Sundays. In response, the city sent in hundreds of police to enforce the ban. When faced with this intrusion to their freedom of expression, the entire Greenwich community rose as one and protested. They marched and held demonstrations, and were met with violent force to stop them, but they persisted." He smiled and said, "There is one story about the time that I particularly like. One Sunday the people of the Village were in the park and faced with a line of battle-ready police. They knew that if they sang there would be violent retribution."

He looked up and asked the class, "Do you know what they did?" He saw some heads shaking from side to side and said, "They sang the American National Anthem, and of course the police could do nothing. The irony is that the American anthem ends with the line: O'er land of the free and the home of the brave!

They eventually won their right to sing on Sundays, so what actually is the point I am trying to make? The point is that what the Beat movement did in New York in 1961 was to hold up a mirror to society and stop the erosion of their right to freedom of speech. They did this as a generation, and they sent out this message to the rest of the world as one."

He looked around at all in the class, and his tone changed to one of anger. "We are all of us fourteen years old, and are becoming a generation in the same way as the beats were a generation. It is our right – no, it is much more than a right – it is our duty to hold up a mirror to society." He pointed around the room and said, "We will all of us become a part of the establishment in time, but before we do, we must sing our own song. We must fight anyone that tells us that we cannot sing it. If we do not do this, then we will not have played our part."

He was silent for a while and said, "That is what I have learned from New York." There was not a sound as he looked at the class. Some of them had very puzzled expressions on their faces. He jumped down off the table and simply said as he walked out of the classroom, "But then again, New York is not for everyone."

Conor was sitting on a bench in the schoolyard when Miss Martin and Melanie came over and sat down at either side of him.

"Melanie just told me about you moving to Ireland," the teacher said. "I am really sorry to hear that." She put her hand on his shoulder and said, "That turned into a bit of a speech back there."

Conor looked at her and said, "That is how I feel. I don't expect anyone to get what I am saying, but I feel compelled to say it."

The teacher smiled at him with real warmth and said, "Oh, for sure I get it, and I am sure that this lady gets it too. Just to let you know, I was living in Greenwich Village in 1961 and marched to the square." She said this with real pride in her voice, "I still have the scars to prove it."

He sat upright and looked her, "Were you? Will you tell me about it?"

She smiled and said, "Someday maybe."

Melanie nudged the boy with her elbow and said quietly, "Show off." The three of them laughed and it lightened the mood considerably. The teacher looked at the two youngsters and something seemed to dawn on her. She asked, "I expect that this move to Ireland is not exactly greeted with great joy by either of you then?" And she looked at each of them in turn.

The two muttered "No," together.

"When do you leave, Conor?"

"Next Sunday," he said.

"Oh God, that soon?"

They sat in silence for a little while and then the teacher looked at the boy warmly and said, "I am really sad to see you go. You know your presentation in there was well over the top. It was brilliant, but it was well over the top."

He looked at her with an expression that was very serious and said, "It was meant to be well over the top, Miss."

The teacher said, "God, I am so going to miss you. I had better get back into the class." As she was getting up she said, "After that speech, they could be starting a riot," and she left the two on the bench. She stopped as she was halfway across the yard and looked back at them. What she saw was not the brilliance she had come to associate with these two youngsters, but just a pair of really sad fourteen-year-olds.

She walked back towards them, and said, "Melanie, can you come here for a minute?"

The girl got up and made her way over to the teacher and asked, "What, Miss?"

The teacher looked at her directly and said, "Is there something going on here between you two that shouldn't be?"

The girl looked at her, then over to where the boy was sitting on the bench and back to the teacher and said, in a slightly sharp voice, "Absolutely not, Miss."

The teacher got the sense that the girl was disappointed that she would ask this.

"I am sorry, Melanie, but I had to ask."

"I understand, Miss," she said and her voice softened. "We are connected in a fundamental way. Sometimes when he speaks it is as if I am speaking. He can be infuriatingly clever, but he is very honest and we see the world in the same way."

The girl smiled a little shyly and said, "I do like him too though."

The teacher smiled, looked directly at the girl and said, "I have an idea. My flat is down on Ladbroke Grove and if you two wanted to use it one evening before Conor goes, maybe to cook a meal and have a chat, you would be welcome."

Melanie smiled at the teacher and said, "That would be really lovely."

"I am going out on Friday evening and I won't be back until about half past nine. The flat is at 141D Ladbroke Grove, just beside the entrance to the tube station." She handed the girl two keys out of her pocket. "I have a set of spare keys here, one is for the main door, and the other is for the flat on the top floor. I have a record player if you want to bring some music."

The girl's expression turned a little sad and she said, "It is all changing, you know."

"Yes I know, but treasure these times." She gave the girl a warm hug.

"All right, then, I will see the two of you at about half past nine on Friday when I get back." With that she left them and walked back into the classroom.

Melanie turned to the boy and asked, "Do you want to walk me down to Ladbroke Grove?"

He nodded and they got up and headed out of the schoolyard. As they went out through the gate she caught his hand and held it tightly.

"You know what, Conor?"

"What?"

"I fancy going to Speakers' Corner tomorrow." She stopped to ask him, "It is on Sunday that they do the speaking, right?"

"Yes," said the boy.

"Are you on, Conor?"
"Always," he said.

Chapter 23

It was early on Sunday morning and the two youngsters were walking past Marble Arch at the end of Oxford Street. They had taken the train from Ladbroke Grove to Paddington and walked from there towards Park Lane. They entered the corner of the park where the speakers gather to stand on their boxes and give their view of the world every Sunday morning. Conor had explained to the girl that this tradition had been going on for centuries and this was where devout religious and political activists, contrarians and just plain loonies went to vent their spleen.

As they entered Speakers' Corner, a fine crowd had gathered around the dozen or so speakers that were scattered about. Near the entrance there was a large black man in flowing white robes. On his head was a pillbox hat embroidered with gold, and a group had gathered around him. He was a giant of a man and standing on his box made him look bigger still. He looked around the group of people and swept a pointed finger at everyone and in a booming voice said, "If ye want to escape the wrath of God ye must repent on thy knees and pray for forgiveness. For if ye do not repent, ye will burn in hell for all eternity." With eyes blazing he said, "Ye stand before me, the scum of the earth. Beg for His forgiveness or I will have Him smite thee with His mighty sword. Ye that are Satan's progeny."

Conor looked at the girl and said, "I think we are in deep trouble here." She smiled at him and they moved on. There was a man ahead of them that had a larger crowd gathered around him. He was halfway up a stepladder and the two youngsters stood towards the back of the crowd. The man was quite short and chubby with a big fat face that seemed to have no neck attached. He wore a white suit with a white bowler hat and a union John patterned waistcoat. A white bulldog was tied to the bottom of the step ladder and the dog was lying down with his face resting on his front paws.

The man had a strong cockney accent and spoke very loudly.

He asked the crowd, "What is London?" And looked around him at the faces that were looking up at him.

"It is a city that is made up of multiple ethnic groups working side by side with a common purpose to achieve their goals of prosperity and happiness."

He looked around and asked, "Is that right?"

The crowd murmured, "Yes."

Raising his voice, he asked again, "Is that right?"

The crowd said, "Yes," a little more loudly.

The man took the bowler hat off his head and looking down at the ground, he shouted, "Is that right?"

More loudly the crowd said, "Yes," in response.

The man swept his hat in a large arc and shouted, "No, it is not fucking right. England and this city of London belongs to the English. I don't go to your countries to live, so why should you come here to mine?"

The crowd were taken aback by the pronouncement.

The man let out a long sigh and climbed up another step. He

SONGS *and* PORTOBELLOS

put back on his hat, and in a soft voice he asked the crowd, "Do we have anyone here from Northern Ireland?"

There were a couple of faint "Yeses," from the crowd.

The man smiled at them and said again in a soft and friendly tone, "From Northern Ireland, are you? Whereabouts?"

Two men in the crowd said, "Belfast."

He smiled at the two men and said, "Ah yes, Belfast, by the Lagan."

The man looked away from the two men and just said, "Belfast, Belfast, Belfast."

Very suddenly he snapped back to look at them and shouted "Why do you want to kill each other? Are you fucking mad?"

The crowd became more uncomfortable and they were beginning to mutter objections to the comments. You could see that the man on the ladder was enjoying himself and revelled in the discomfort of the crowd. He leaned on the ladder and said, "What you have to understand is that it is all very simple. Northern Ireland belongs to Éire."

There was a gasp from the crowd.

With his finger pointing to the ground and moving up and down in rhythm to his words, he said, "And Éire belongs to Great Britain."

This was met with some more voices of disapproval, but they were also mixed with some ripples of laughter.

Conor looked at Melanie, and he could see that she had turned pale.

"Are you OK?" he asked.

She looked at him and said, "You know some people believe that stuff. I cannot let this go unchallenged," and she moved forward towards the man.

Conor followed her and stood by her side.

She said, "Excuse me," to the man.

The man looked down and smiling said, "What can I do for you, love?"

"You are a fascist pig."

The man looked at her still smiling and said, "Ah, look at her. Isn't she lovely?" He shrugged his shoulders and said, "What makes you think that your opinion is of any interest to me or to anyone?"

She replied, "Of course it isn't of interest to you, because you are too stupid and ignorant to understand anything, you mindless idiot."

The crowd turned to the girl and there were some shouts of approval.

The man looked at the crowd and pointing to the girl he said, "You see what our wonderful multi-ethnic society is raising." He stared directly at her and pointing to his chest said, "You forget that it was me and my likes that fought to keep this country free. If it were not for us you would be speaking German."

Conor turned to look at the girl and he could see her eyes were blazing.

She smiled at the man and said, "Is that all you have to say? Is that the only contribution that you can make? I pity you. England would be well served if you would just crawl back under whatever rock you came out from." The crowd were now openly voicing their approval.

The man said in a calm voice, "Listen, I don't blame you. I blame the foreign influences in this country that have turned you against your own country. You have forgotten what it means to be English."

The crowd raised their voice in disapproval at the comments, and then turned to the girl for her reaction. She looked at him and smiled, "You know what, I feel sorry for you. But I feel worse for the people that have stopped here to listen to the crass ranting of an idiot with the brain of an amoeba. You understand nothing about being English and you only have a warped notion of nationalism that you have formed in your own narrow little mind." At this stage the crowd cheered and applauded. After that, everything that the man tried to say in response was drowned out by the crowd with jeering and boos. Melanie turned to Conor, linked his arm and said with a smile, "Come on, let's go," and they strolled away from the group.

They walked slowly away from Speakers' Corner to where it was quiet, and found an unoccupied bench. As they sat down they were approached by a squirrel, who turned sideways to them and sized them up with his large dark eye and then ran off into the park.

She looked at the boy and said, "I regret letting him have it, you know, and I do actually feel sorry for him."

"Don't feel sorry," the boy said.

"Maybe I let fly at him because of my own frustration." She paused and said, "You know, because of your news yesterday?"

"Yes, I took a walk after I had heard it on Friday night and kind of let rip myself."

"Who to?" she asked.

"Just at the night sky," he said.

They sat and chatted for a while, and just as they were getting up to leave, the man in the white suit and bowler hat came walking towards them carrying the step ladder, with his dog on a lead. As he came nearer, the dog pulled him over to the two youngsters and he put his paws on the bench looking for attention. Melanie put her hands behind the dog's ears and tickled him. The man said, "I am really sorry. He is always looking for attention. Great turn out today, wasn't it?"

The two nodded.

"Come on Monty, let's go and get a bite of lunch," and the dog jumped down as soon as he heard the word lunch. The man smiled broadly and said, "Good luck to you both. See you next Sunday, I hope," and the man and dog trotted off. As he was leaving he called back over his shoulder and said, "Hope we get as big a crowd next week."

Melanie looked puzzled and turned to the boy, "What did you make of that? It was as if nothing happened back there." Conor looked at the figures of the man and his dog disappearing into the distance, and, smiling, turned to her and said, "I have been coming here for a few years now, and I see it as a theatre."

The girl looked at him and said, "Go on."

"What went on back there," and he pointed to the spot where the man had his ladder, "was a performance, like a small play."

She looked up to the sky and said, "And I was one of the performers. God, I feel so stupid."

"Don't," said the boy. "You gave the play meaning."

"But what about him?" and she pointed to the man with the ladder and the dog going through the gate. "Do you think he believes in that racist rubbish? Or is he just an actor?"

"I don't know if he believes it or not, but I expect that whatever he believes, one thing is for sure and that is, that he is lonely," said the boy.

"I see what you mean." She looked at him and smiled, "You can be a real clever clogs at times, you know that, Conor?"

They got up and started towards Park Lane and Conor looked at her and laughing said, "The brain of an amoeba – where do you get them from?"

She laughed as they strolled out of the park, and were watched all the way by the squirrel as they passed.

Chapter 24

The week flew by, and the boy and girl managed to fit in as much as possible into every day. They paid visits to many places that she had not yet seen, like the Victoria and Albert Museum, Buckingham Place and Regents Park. They even went on a boat tour of the Thames, which was something the boy had never done before. He enjoyed the girl's company so much that for the time being he was able to put his impending move to Ireland into the back of his mind.

On the Thursday morning they had visited the tower of London and seen the Crown Jewels. Conor could sense that the girl was not at all impressed by this display of wealth. It was now the afternoon, and they were sitting in the usual coffee shop beside Ladbroke Grove tube station. Melanie had told him earlier in the week about the evening at Miss Martin's, and they were chatting about their plans for the coming Friday evening.

Conor said, "It has just occurred to me that tomorrow evening will be the last chance we have to meet up before I head away."

"What about Saturday?" she asked.

"I have to help out with packing the stuff for shipping, and a load of other jobs I expect, so I don't see how I can get away."

She paused, looked away, and then back to him and said, "Does that mean you won't be coming to the school to hear my project presentation either?"

"God, I had not thought of that." He could see she was unhappy and he said, "I have an idea. Why don't you bring it to Miss Martin's flat and give me the presentation in person."

The girl beamed and asked, "Would that be OK?"

"It would be most excellent," the boy replied.

"What else would you like to do tomorrow evening?" he asked her.

"I was thinking about that, and I was wondering if we should cook a meal."

"Can you cook?" he asked.

"Are you joking?" she said with a grin.

"OK, I will take that as a strong yes then."

But what will we cook? She thought as she took a sip of her tea. She looked at him and said, "How about a curry?"

"Sounds great to me."

The girl drummed her nails on the table and said out loud to herself, "I wonder if Miss Martin is a vegetarian. I wouldn't want to cook meat in her flat, just in case. Maybe I could do a vegetable curry."

"Vegetable curry it is then," said the boy.

Melanie took out a note book and wrote out two lists of ingredients, one for him and the other for her.

She said, "I will bring the spices and rice, and you can get the vegetables – just make sure they are very fresh. And oh yes, bring the bottle of wine we have left over."

"Are you going to give the wine a lash then, Melanie?"

She laughed and said, "Can you imagine how bad I'd be

if I was drunk. That guy in Hyde Park would be swinging off his ladder."

He smiled at her and said, "Wine is off the menu for you then."

She smiled and said, "Bring it anyway, unless you are scared."

He looked at her, "I am very much afraid, but I will bring it despite that. That is what they call courage."

"OK, then let's split up and get the bits and pieces – and remember, make sure everything is fresh," and she tore out the page from her notebook and handed it to him.

They finished their drinks and left the coffee shop. She went up Ladbroke Grove and he went towards the convenience store on the corner of Westbourne Park Road.

He strolled the hundred yards or so down the road and stood in front of the vegetables that were displayed along the outside wall of the shop. They were all lined up in shallow wicker baskets. Mindful of the girl's warning, he was being very choosy. The baskets of vegetables were propped up at an angle to make it easy to select, and he had carrots, onions, apples and mushrooms in separate brown paper bags. When he was done, he picked up the paper bags and went into the shop to pay for them.

Behind the counter was the red-faced man in the brown shop coat. He weighed each bag on the white scales that sat on the counter. The face of the scales was triangular and printed on the face were rows of prices. The furthest column to the left was cost-per-pound. When the needle settled on the weight, the man ran his finger across from the cost-per-pound to where the needle intersected the row and this gave him the price. With each bag he repeated the performance and rang up the till with the amount. When he had finished, he rang up the total, which came to three shillings and nine pence.

As Conor was counting out the money the man said, "No girlfriend with you today then, son?"

The boy stopped and said, "What?"

The shopkeeper repeated, "I said you don't have your girlfriend with you today."

The boy paused and said, "No."

Having paid for the vegetables, he left the shop and started to walk back towards Kensal Road.

As he walked he thought to himself: Girlfriend?

It was Friday and he was getting ready for the evening with Melanie. They had decided to meet at six o'clock at Miss Martin's flat, and he had laid out his denim jacket and beige cords on the bed with his navy round-neck sweater. As he looked at the clothes, he thought that jeans and jackets reach a stage when they are just perfect. When they are new they are hard and stiff and not nice at all, and when they were old they became thin and had no shape. To him this jacket and jeans were at the perfect stage. He wondered how long they stayed at this peak of perfection, and thought, perhaps only a couple of weeks. On the bed alongside his clothes was the LP of Paul Simon that he had bought in Shepherd's Bush and some singles he had selected from his record collection. Beside this were the vegetables for the curry, and the spare bottle of red wine that he had brought up from the Portobello. He carefully placed all the items into a brown paper carrier bag.

Every afternoon during the week, the boy had gone to Washington Square, but there had been no sign of John. He was concerned about the man and hoped that he would meet him before he had to leave. The boy's parents were in a frenzy of activity getting everything packed and ready for the trip to

Ireland. His father told him the plan was they were going to drive to Holyhead in North Wales, and then take the Mail Boat to Dun Laoghaire in Dublin. The more he thought about it, the more depressed he became.

He had decided earlier in the day that he would go to New York and check on John again before he met up with Melanie. He put on his clothes and left the carrier bag where it was on the bed, to be collected after his visit to New York. He checked himself out in the long mirror in the bathroom. He had taken a bath earlier and washed his hair. His hair reached down to where his neck joined his shoulders and it was very dark and shone brightly from the washing. Brushing it would do nothing to put it in order, so he just let it take its own path. He raced out of the flat and within minutes he was walking on Bleecker Street towards Washington Square. As he entered the square, he could see the bench where John normally sat and saw that it was empty. Turning around he decided that he would go to The Preacher and see if John was there.

He skipped down the steps and into the pub. There was a young girl cleaning the tables. She was very pretty with shoulder-length hair that was a beautiful shade of auburn. She turned around to look at him, and he could see immediately the resemblance to Tony.

He looked at her and asked, "You are not by any chance Kathy, are you?"

"Every chance," she said. "And judging from your accent you must be Conor."

They shook hands and she said, "My father has told me about you. He calls you the English kid with the blue eyes and all the questions."

"That's me," Conor said. "Is Tony around?"

"Yes, sure – He is out the back, I will get him for you."

Within a minute Tony came through the door and said, "Hey, Conor, how's it going. Fancy a soda or a cup of coffee?"

He then turned to the girl and said, "Have you met Kathy?"

"Hi Tony – yes, we made our introductions," and he smiled at the girl. "I am OK for coffee, thank you. I was just trying to catch up with John, and I was wondering if you have seen him around at all?"

Tony looked closely at the boy and said, "The big man is in hospital getting something sorted out."

He could see immediately that the boy was concerned and he added, "By all accounts it is not too serious. He comes in most evenings when he is around, so when he comes again I will tell him you were looking for him, OK?"

"Thanks Tony, it is just that I leave on Sunday, and I wanted to catch up with him before I go."

"I am sorry to hear that you're leaving us, you have brightened up the old place." He paused and said, "When I see John, I will let him know. He holds you in very high regard you know, which is good enough for me anytime." He reached across the counter and shook the boy's hand. "It has been a real pleasure and come in to see the old Preacher anytime you are in town."

He put his arm around the girl and said, "Kathy here is going to help me next summer in the bar. She is saving for college, so she expects to make fortune."

"That is great, Tony," and Conor turned to the girl and said, "You do know that this is the best coffee anywhere in New York?"

The girl smiled back at him and said, "So he keeps telling me."

"OK, then I had better get going, many thanks Tony and Kathy," and he left the bar and went back out onto the street.

He strolled back towards the Portobello with John on his

mind. He hoped that the man was going to be OK, and that he would get a chance to say goodbye to him. He entered through the door on Bleecker Street, closed it behind him and made his way onto the stage to sit down at the table. The Portobello looked beautiful. The sun shone in the window through the opaque glass and lit up the place. Every piece of brass and mirror glittered. Soon all this would be gone and replaced with what, he did not know. But he thought to himself that this is Friday evening and he was going to spend it with Melanie. He smiled when he thought of her, and he could not think of a single minute that he had spent with her over the summer that he did not enjoy. He got off the stage and made his way to the flat upstairs.

Chapter 25

When he got back into the flat it was half past five, so he reckoned he would start making his way down to Ladbroke Grove. He gathered the records, wine and groceries and stepped out onto Kensal Road. As he walked he thought to himself that his attention all week was focused on how much he would miss the Portobello, Melanie and John. As he looked around at the street and the old iron railway bridge, he realised that this street had been a part of his life too, and would also be deeply missed. Down along the road he could see that the pubs were already packed, as they were at this time every Friday. As he passed the Tavistock, he had to make his way through the men with Irish accents that had spilled out onto the pavement.

They all seemed to be huge men, and their pints of beer seemed to disappear in their fists. In some ways they were terrifying, but he had noticed that when they were sober they spoke very softly. He successfully navigated his way past the pub and passed the Parish Church of Saint Michael. Seeing the church reminded him of when he was very young, asking his mother if they could go in and look at it, and she just said, "No" without any explanation. His mother's reluctance to go inside meant that as he got a bit older he was driven to see the inside of the church for himself. When he did eventually go inside, he found it a dark and gloomy building and nothing special. He eventually came to the conclusion that she did not want to go into the building because it was a Protestant church. He asked her if this was so, and she said it would be more in his line if he went to mass on Sundays rather than asking questions like that.

As he passed the entrance to the tube station, he checked the door numbers, 147, 145, 143 and then 141. Climbing up the steps he checked the buzzers by the side of the door and he saw "Ann Martin 141D". He turned around and sat on the steps waiting for Melanie to arrive, and it was not long before he saw her coming around the corner from Lancaster Road.

She wore the same black dress that she had on the first day that he had seen her at school, but with a broad-rimmed, black hat. He thought she looked beautiful and when she got to the step he said, "You look great."

She left down her shopping bag and said, "Why, thank you, you don't look so bad yourself." She held up the brim of her hat with one hand and gave him a warm hug. They entered the building which was quite dark inside, and they carried their bags up the four flights of stairs to the top floor. At the top of the landing was a white door with 141D in brass letters on it. Melanie opened the door and the two found themselves in a room that was full of little tables, high-backed wicker chairs, a small sofa and a bean bag in the corner. A small dining-room table with two chairs sat under a window that looked down on the busy street. Everywhere around the walls were shelves stuffed full of books and Indian ornaments. Anywhere there was any wall space hung a painting. The paintings were mostly impressionist style, and were a mixture of originals and prints.

Directly opposite the dining table and chairs was an opening into a small kitchen. The kitchen did not have a door, but it had a type of curtain made up of little pieces of bamboo on long strings that parted as you walked through. It made a kind of musical sound as the bamboo beads bounced off each other as you passed. Scattered all around the floor were brightly patterned afghan rugs.

The two went into the kitchen and left their groceries on the counter beside the sink. The kitchen had that beautiful smell of fresh coffee and garlic. They went back through the bamboo curtain into the living room, and Melanie looked around the room and said, "I love this place. It is exactly how I imagined it would be." They set about making themselves at home. Conor lit the jasmine incense stick and candle that was on the table and then switched on the little table lamps that were around the living room. He found two wine glasses, opened the bottle of red wine and poured them both a glass. They clinked their glasses and said, "Cheers."

They sipped the wine and she asked, "What do you think?"

"Of what?" he asked.

"The wine."

"Honestly?"

"Yes," she said.

He made a face and said loudly, "Yuck."

She put her glass down on the table and bent over with laughter, "God, it is awful, isn't it?"

"Come on then," she said, "let's get started with the cooking. Will you find the record player first and put on some music?"

The stereo was in the corner and he turned it on. As it was warming up, he took the LP from its sleeve and placed it onto the turntable of the stereo. He lifted the needle arm from its rest and the turntable started revolving. Very carefully, he placed the needle on the space before the first track. A little crackle could be heard at first, and then the beautiful clear guitar at the beginning of 'I Am a Rock'. He adjusted the volume so that the music filled the room but was not too loud, and he got up to join the girl in the kitchen.

They started preparing the meal with the girl as cook and the boy as helper. Conor's job was to wash the vegetables and do whatever else he was told. First an onion was peeled, chopped and thrown into a large pot that the girl had heating with a little olive oil. The onion was cooked slowly, and two cloves of garlic and a small amount of ginger were also peeled, chopped and then thrown into the pot with the onion. The boy washed two carrots with a green pepper and some mushrooms, which were placed on the chopping board for the girl.

As the vegetables were arriving, the girl chopped them and added them to the mixture in the pot. The room was filling up with the smell of onion and garlic frying. A chopped up apple was added to the vegetables and stirred into the pot. Out of her shopping bag, Melanie took three spice jars, cumin, garam masala and turmeric, along with a small red chilli. She split and deseeded the chilli, chopped it finely and added it to the pot off the back of her knife. Taking each spice jar in turn, she sprinkled some of the contents onto a teaspoon and then added it to the half-full pot of vegetables. She stirred it all together and salt and pepper were added. Under the girl's close scrutiny, Conor opened a can of tomatoes and she added the contents to the pot. She dipped her little finger into the mixture and tasted it. She added another pinch of salt and pepper with a little sugar and she declared, "Done," and she turned down the heat. "That will take about forty-five minutes."

A large bunch of coriander was produced from the girl's bag, rinsed under the cold tap and dried on a tea towel before it was finely chopped. This was left on the chopping board. "Now," the girl said, "Let's do the rice." Out of the shopping bag came a bag of basmati rice, and she filled a large cup with the rice and poured it into a fine strainer. The strainer was placed into a pot and left under the cold tap with the water running. The pot filled up with water, but the strainer was higher, so the water escaped through the strainer above the rim of the pot. This meant that the water was constantly changing and the rice swirled around in the bottom of the strainer.

After a few minutes the girl turned off the tap and said, "OK, let the rice soak for a little while and we can cook it in about thirty minutes. It only takes about ten minutes to cook. Do you want to sit and chat?" she asked.

"I'd love to," he said. He was mesmerised by how quickly and efficiently she worked. As he looked around the kitchen he could see that everything had been tidied as she went along."

They went out into the dining room and sat down together on the little couch. Just as they sat down, 'Most Peculiar Man' started to play on the stereo.

The girl spoke, "What do you think, Conor?"

"About what?" he asked.

"OK, Conor," – she paused – and looking at the wall in front of her, she said, "I find myself thinking about you a lot when we are not with each other and that really upsets me, because now you are leaving."

He looked at her and said, "I do know what you mean."

The LP had just finished. He took it off the turntable and placed it on top of its album cover. He picked up the singles, took them out of their sleeves and stacked them on the turntable spindle. He moved the arm across and placed it on top of the small stack of records. He changed the speed to 45 rpm, and pulled down the start switch. The turntable started spinning and after a little whirring noise the first single dropped onto the rubber mat. He waited to see the needle arm come across, position itself over the start of the record and slowly move onto the record surface. The organ opening of 'A Whiter Shade of Pale' filled the room.

He sat down again, and he noticed for the first time since they had met they were a little awkward around each other, so they just sat in silence and listened to the music.

When 'A Whiter Shade of Pale' ended, the next record dropped down, and 'Waterloo Sunset' started to play. Conor stood up from the couch and held out his hand, "May I have the pleasure?"

She turned her head to the side and looking away from him, said, "No thanks."

He sat straight down feeling a little embarrassed, and she laughed, "God, you give up easily don't you?" and she caught his hand and pulled him up. She put her arms around his neck and lightly held her cheek against his as they danced slowly to the music.

He put his hands on either side of her waist, and he could get the scent of apples from her hair. When the line "Terry meets Julie" came on, he pulled his head back and looked at her. Slowly their lips met and they kissed in a very gentle way as they danced to the music. They kissed all the way through to the end of the song, and then they moved apart, sat down, and were silent again.

They continued to sit in silence for a little while.

Eventually he said, "Do you think that changes things?"

She smiled at him and said, "No, that was just another beautiful moment in a beautiful summer."

They sat and listened to some more of the music and then she said, "Come on then, 'Terry', let's cook the rice."

Chapter 26

Melanie took the strainer with rice from the pot, and emptied the water out. She wiped the bottom of the pot with a tea towel, and dumped the contents of the strainer into it. Then taking the same cup that she had used to measure the rice, she added two cupfuls of cold water with a pinch of salt and put it on a high heat. While they were waiting for the water to boil, she took three plates and put them under the grill.

Turning around she looked at the boy. He was leaning against the counter looking at her.

"What are you thinking about?"

"This summer."

She smiled at him, "It has been wonderful, hasn't it?" she said.

"What happens now then? Is that it – just memories?"

She stopped what she was doing and said, "I remember clearly what John said in the Portobello. He said that when you lose someone that is close to you, you take the things that you admire about them, like courage and character and put them with your own. That way, the spirit that sets them apart, lives on within you."

She looked at him and smiling said, "This summer has brought us together, and much more than memories, you are now within me, Conor, and I within you, and nothing can ever change that, wherever we are."

The boy just smiled at her. "OK, Melanie, but I got the better part of the deal."

She smiled at him, "For sure you did."

After a little while, almost all of the water had evaporated from the rice, so she turned off the heat and placed a tea towel over the lid. The grill was turned on over the plates to warm them up and she said, "Right then, Conor, let's set the table." This took a little time as they were not familiar with the kitchen, but they found a tablecloth and cutlery and set them out on the small table. Although they had not touched them, the two glasses of red wine were set out also.

She turned to him and said, "Conor, will you switch off some of the table lamps and put on some more music?"

He switched off all except one of the lamps, took off the singles, and put on side two of the Paul Simon LP.

They went back into the kitchen and the plates were taken out from under the grill using the tea towel and placed onto the counter. The girl put out the rice onto the three plates with a little hollow in the middle of each and into this she spooned the curry mixture.

"Who is the third plate for?" he asked.

"I thought it would be nice to save some for Miss Martin."

"Nice thought," he said.

The chopped green coriander was sprinkled over the curries and from her bag she took out some flat bread and a little jar of chutney.

He looked at her and asked, "What exactly do you keep in that bag?"

She laughed and said, "The essentials, naan bread and apple chutney."

"Apple chutney – where did you get that?"

"I made it."

"You really are the complete overachiever, you know that?"

"Well, obviously," she said as she held her hand out in front of her and looked at her nails.

Within a very short while they were sitting at the table eating the curry and mopping up the sauce with chunks of naan bread.

Every morsel of the curry was eaten, and was washed down with two tall glasses of water which they had substituted for the red wine.

Conor said, "You know, I have never had a curry before, and that was just delicious, thank you."

She smiled and said, "You are very welcome."

They looked across the table at each other. Neither of them said anything, but they got up at the same time and started clearing away. In the kitchen he washed and she dried, and they made sure that everything was spotless. Melanie had kept a piece of the naan bread, and put it with the plate for Miss Martin, and then she covered the plate with some tinfoil and placed it in the fridge. They decided that they would pour their glasses of wine back into the bottle. When this was done, Conor pushed the top of the cork back into it and left it on the counter for Miss Martin.

It had turned dark outside, but they kept just the one table lamp on, along with the candle on the table. They had returned to the couch and 'Kathy's Song' was playing. She rested her head on his shoulder.

They sat in silence for a little while and he asked, "What about giving me your presentation on London?"

She sat upright and said, "Do you really want to hear it?"

He got up and turned down the stereo, and as he sat back down he said, "It is the only reason I came."

She grinned and went to her bag and brought out some immaculately written notes.

He smiled at her, and she asked, "What are you smiling at?"

"Everything about you is perfection, isn't it?"

She laughed and said, "You should see me when I really get angry, perfection goes out the window and I start swearing like a sailor."

She stood up in front of him and started, "To the tourist, London has visible links to its history. Ancient buildings not only still exist but are used in the everyday life of the city. The Houses of Parliament, Westminster Abbey and the Bank of England are prime examples of where London displays its aura of permanence. When visitors come, they get a visual excursion into the past, and I expect also a strong sense of nostalgia. A nice example of this link with history is the Blackwall Tunnel under the Thames. If you drive through the tunnel you will find it doesn't go straight, but rather it zigzags a number of times. The reason for this, is to make ascent and decent more gradual and therefore gentler on the horses that used to pull the carts and to prevent them from bolting when they saw daylight."

"Is that right?" Conor asked.

"Yes," she said, "and don't interrupt."

"Sorry," he said and he smiled at her.

She paused, "At the heart of London is the City of Westminster, which is quite small. It is a little more than eight square miles and has a population of less than 200,000. At one time it was the commercial capital of the world and the centre of a powerful empire, but this is no longer the case. It is still powerful, but it has ceded a lot of this power to the US, Europe and Asia. However, it is still the centre of the commonwealth.

A vast British Empire grew from the colonization of other countries down the centuries. The process of colonization was for strategic, military and economic reasons, and brought vast wealth and power with it. Evidence of this colonization can be seen in the ethnic groups that are now part of the population, from India, the West Indies and Asia. The brief for this summer project was to provide an insight into London's culture and society. I have had the advantage of being able to look at this first hand, whereas the rest of the class have had to use their imagination. I found it challenging though, as a culture is not openly visible just by looking at buildings and talking to people. It is my view, that to understand culture you need to observe how people interact with each other, and what is the structure of the society in which they live."

She paused for a little, "When you look at the people of London, there are a number of classes. The layers of these classes are too diverse to detail, but they relate to wealth, ethnic origin and colour. All of these class levels coexist, but the tiers of society are isolated from each other. At the top of these class tiers are the wealthy white English, and at the bottom are the poor from the West Indies or Africa. However, if you look at this in finer detail even the wealthy white English are not the ruling class. This position is reserved for royalty. A monarchy is not uncommon throughout the world, but is the very definition of a class-led society. The monarch is not elected, but has the highest class position in society by virtue of birthright. The wealthiest people in London are not considered to be ruling class unless they become associated with the monarch."

She again paused, "In this regard, there is a tradition that the monarch awards honours to successful people through knighthoods and various other titles. To the observer this may appear to raise the successful into the ruling class by recognising their achievements. As I have thought about it more, however, I cannot help but wonder if it might be the reverse and that the monarchy is in fact rewarding itself with the success of others. To conclude, London is a complex mixture of tradition, class, culture and efficiency. I moved here just four months ago, and I have to make a clear statement that I do not agree with its class structure, but I have already formed a love for the city and its people." She paused and said, "But not all of its people."

She concluded with, "I have written a London guide for key places to visit, and I will leave it with my essay in 'The City Library' here in the school."

Conor said, "Did you really write a London guide?"

"Yes of course. What did you think?"

"I thought it was powerful, honest and highly opinionated. In other words – perfect."

She smiled at him and said, "I knew you would like it," and she sat down beside him.

They sat in silence for another little while, and then she asked, "What did you think the first time you saw me?"

"I thought you were perfect, even your bony knees."

She jumped up and looked down at her knees and said, "God, they are bony, aren't they?"

"Yes," he said, "but perfect."

She said, "I really loved meeting with John. Even though we only spoke together for a short while, I feel that he touched my life. Is that why you wanted me to meet him?"

The boy thought for a little while and said, "You know, I think that is probably true. I wanted you to learn from him what I have learned." Conor then looked a little sombre and continued, "The word at the moment though, is that he is in hospital."

She sat upright and said, "Oh, I so hope he is OK. He is a very special man. Will you get a chance to meet with him before you go?"

"I hope so," said the boy.

They both turned as they heard the key in the door.

Chapter 27

Into the flat walked Miss Martin. She smiled at the boy and girl and said, "Hello, you two." They said together, "Hello, Miss."

She looked different than at school, with her jeans and black waistcoat over a long white collarless shirt. She wore a black beret and her silky blond hair was loosely tied up under it.

She left down her satchel on the chair beside the door, and asked, "Well, did you have a nice time?"

"Great," they both said together.

"Something smells lovely. What did you cook?"

"We had a curry," said the girl.

She said, "I am sorry I did not get you to keep me a little. I am starving. I haven't eaten since lunchtime."

Melanie said, "We did, Miss. It is in the fridge."

"My pair of heroes," the teacher said with a grin. "Let me get it heated up, and I can eat while we chat."

The teacher went into the kitchen, took the plate from the fridge and emptied the contents into a pot. She took out the naan bread and put it in a bowl that she heated under the grill. She stirred the contents of the pot all together while it was heating, and saw the bottle of wine on the counter.

She stuck her head through the bamboo curtain and said, "Were you two drinking wine?"

The two youngsters looked at each other and laughed, and Conor said, "We took a sip, but couldn't stand it, so we put it back in the bottle and left it for you." The boy paused and said, "That didn't come out quite right, Miss, but I hope you know what I mean."

The teacher laughed and said, "Yes, I do."

The girl said, "I have left some chutney along with some chopped coriander in the fridge if you would like some."

"Perfect," said the teacher and disappeared behind the bamboo curtain.

She reappeared a few minutes later carrying a steaming bowl with a spoon in one hand and a glass of wine in the other.

She sat cross-legged to one side of them in a tall wicker chair, with the bowl in her hands and the glass of wine on a small table beside her.

After a couple of spoonfuls she said, "This is really delicious. Did you two make this?"

"Melanie did," said the boy.

"Where did you get the chutney? What is in it?"

"It is apple chutney and I made it myself," said the girl.

"Well done to you. It is lovely."

They sat and chatted while Miss Martin ate her food and drank her glass of wine. When she had finished the food, she just said, "Delicious, thank you," and dropped the bowl out to the kitchen. She came back into the room and sat down on the wicker chair again.

"I was out at the local amateur dramatic society, or am-dram as I call it. They are thinking of putting on a play in the summer and we had a planning meeting this evening to consider what to put on."

"Did they decide on a play, Miss?" asked the girl.

"Yes, one of the members knows a director that has worked with the Royal Shakespeare. He thinks that he can get her to direct, and if she agrees we are going to put on *As You Like It*. The teacher looked at the girl and said, "You should come along Melanie, when we get it set up."

The girl beamed. "I would love that."

"I will let you know when everything is sorted out."

They were quiet for a little while as the teacher drank her glass of wine. Conor went out to the kitchen and brought in the bottle and topped up her glass.

The teacher looked at him and said, "What a class act you are, Conor."

He looked at her and said, "Just doing my job, Miss."

Conor said, "You were going to tell us about New York in 1961, Miss."

She smiled at the boy, "Never going to let that one go were you?"

He smiled back and said, "No chance."

The teacher said, "By the way, I know that convention dictates that you call me 'Miss' at school, but I cannot describe how much I hate it, so this side of the fence please call me Ann, OK?"

They both said, "OK."

She smiled to herself and said, "Yes, I was in New York in 1961 and it was a time of great happiness in my life. I left college in '58, and decided to travel. I went first to Europe and took various jobs along the way to keep myself fed, but I tired of it quickly and headed to the Far East. I spent six months in Indonesia, which I loved very much." She looked over at the two and said, "And still do. On my travels I had read a little of the Beat poets and this really appealed to me, so I headed to San Francisco. At that time San Francisco was at the centre of the movement." She paused, looking down at her wine glass and said, "Believe it or not, I hung out with Ginsberg, Ferlinghetti, McClure and even the great Jack Kerouac. It was a very wild time and I was a very wild child."

She took another sip of her wine and looked at the two for a reaction. All she saw was two pairs of eyes fixed on her. "I had heard from one of the group – I can't recall who it was," she paused and said, "It might even have been from Kerouac himself, that Greenwich Village in New York was a great buzz, and to be honest I was getting a little tired of the wildness of San Francisco, so I decided to head for New York. I worked my way across the country travelling mostly by bus, and arrived in New York in the winter of 1959. God, it was so cold. I had never experienced anything like it, but I really loved the place."

She paused and took another sip of wine. "I managed to get a little room in Greenwich on Thompson Street and got a job as a waitress in a coffee shop on Waverley." She turned to the two and said, "I survived a bitterly cold winter, but, despite the cold and not having too much money it was among the happiest times of my life. The people were just beautiful and kind. I knew without doubt that this was the place that I wanted to be. She looked at them and said, "I had found where I belonged."

She continued, "I worked at the coffee shop during the day and I became part of a very close group of friends. We used to hang out at poetry readings and jazz sessions in the Village in the evenings. All of us were in the same boat money-wise, as in continuously broke, but we looked after each other and had a real sense of community."

She looked directly at Melanie and said with a smile, "It

was at one of the jazz sessions that I first met Matthew. He was playing clarinet and I thought he was the most beautiful man I had ever seen."

She looked off into the distance and said, "It was one of those jazz sessions where the jazz would alternate with poetry. When he recited his poems, I could see a passion about him that almost consumed me." She laughed to herself and said, "I had it bad, really bad."

After a pause for another sip of wine she said, "To cut a long story short, we fell in love." She waited for a reaction, but the two just sat absorbing everything that she said. "We dated for a while and had some wonderful times together, and eventually decided to move in together." She paused and asked, "Does that shock you?"

Melanie reached out and touched her hand and said, "It sounds beautiful."

The teacher went on, "I continued to work in the coffee shop and he played his music, wrote poetry and worked by day as a carpenter. We lived in a beautiful little apartment on Bleecker Street, and we had a group of friends that were just wonderful people."

Conor reached over and topped up her wine glass.

"Thank you," she said. "We were inseparable in 1960 and we became almost the iconic representation of the artistic Greenwich couple. Then in 1961 the City started to come the heavy on the Village, and as you said, Conor, they even tried to stop us singing on Sundays in the square."

"Matthew and I sat down, and we pledged to each other that we would do everything we possibly could to stop the erosion of our culture and lifestyle, so we took to protesting and marched to the square. And yes, we sang the 'Star Spangled Banner' and got roughed up by the police, but that only made us more determined." She grew silent and spoke softly, "One morning I got word that Matthew had been badly hurt at a protest. He was in hospital for a while recovering, but unfortunately he had lost most of his hearing due to a beating."

Conor sat upright as his own painful memories came back to him from 1961. The teacher asked him, "Are you OK?"

"Yes, just some memories of my own."

She continued her story, "We believed that he was singled out for a beating by the police, but he never spoke about it," and she smiled to herself saying, "That was his way."

The boy could see tears in her eyes and he looked across at Melanie and he could see tears in hers too. The teacher said, "Well after that, he became colder and more distant. Where there was love before, there was now only bitterness. I did everything I could to bring my Matthew back but he was gone. It broke my heart, but eventually I had to leave New York."

Melanie got up and put her arms around her, and said, "I am so sorry." The teacher put her arm around her and patted her gently on the back and said, "I loved every minute, Melanie."

Conor asked, "He never spoke about the beating?"

"No, we could never get him to talk about it. I always thought that if we could get him to talk, it might have helped him, but we never got him to speak a word about it."

Conor thought about this for a while and said, "And no one saw anything?"

"No, there were all sorts of rumours. There was even a strange person who said that there was the ghost of a small boy standing by his side. But there was nothing that we could put together and use to take on the police with."

The boy hung his head and he fought back his own tears.

"Are you OK, Conor?" asked the teacher.

"Yes," he said. "Like I said – just my own memories."

"Are you going to talk about them?"

He smiled at her and said, "Sometime."

"Anyway, I came back to England and after taking on different jobs here and there, I decided I wanted to become a teacher. I went to teacher training college here in London, and St Charles is my first post. I really did not know what to expect but I am loving it so far. Well, that is my story." She looked at her watch and said, "OK you two, it has been a wonderful evening, and brought back memories to me of beautiful times, but it is time you two were off home."

Chapter 28

Melanie gathered her spices and her hat and Conor put his records together. Soon they were ready to leave.

The boy looked at his teacher and said, "Thank you for sharing your story with us. It must have been very difficult for you to leave New York."

"You have no idea, Conor." She paused and held her head to one side and said to the boy "You know, I never really understood your fascination with that time." She looked at him closely, "A secret maybe?"

"A secret definitely – but a secret that will be told," said the boy.

The teacher put her arms around him and said, "I am going to miss you so much. I see a lot of what I saw in Matthew in you. If you ever get back to London, I have got a lot of friends with spare rooms, so don't worry about where you are going to stay, we will have it covered."

The teacher walked them down the stairs and out of the front door. The two youngsters walked down Ladbroke Grove towards Lancaster Road. They turned and waved goodbye, and the teacher watched them disappear down the road. She stood for a while on the doorstep, and then smiled to herself as she closed the front door.

After leaving the teacher's flat, the two had found a small green area on the corner of St Mark's and Lancaster Road, which was directly opposite Melanie's house. They set down the records and the girl's hat onto a bench and sat down. The streetlights combined with a full moon making it a very bright night.

"I loved the evening," the girl said.

He nodded.

"You know the whole thing with you and 1961?"

"Yes," he said.

"Do you want to tell me?"

"I can't."

She looked at him closely and said, "Do you think you will talk about it someday?"

"Yes I will," he said.

They sat in silence for a while.

"Ann's story was very sad, wasn't it?" the girl said with a sigh.

"It was tragic."

"I wonder what Matthew does now?" she asked.

"I don't know, but I expect an event like that can have a deep impact on your life. But more than the beating and the loss of his hearing, he lost her too."

She looked at him and said, "I never thought of it in that way. He must have been devastated."

"I bet he was."

"It is a big price to pay for singing a song, isn't it?" she said.

He looked at her and said, "But a price worth paying."

She kissed him on the cheek and lay her head on his shoulder.

SONGS *and* PORTOBELLOS

The night was very still and calm. London was very quiet apart from the faint sound of singing coming from the KPH pub on the corner of Ladbroke Grove.

"What are your plans then for tomorrow?" she asked.

"Get stuff packed away, and I want to try to find John to let him know the story about the move to Ireland."

"He means a lot to you, doesn't he?"

"I have been thinking about it, and I see John as sympathetic."

"That is a strange description. How do you mean sympathetic?"

He sat forward with his elbows resting on his knees. "Jack Kerouac once described beat poetry in one word – sympathetic." The boy continued, "For me, I categorise the people in my life as the ones that have sympathy in the Kerouac sense, and those that do not."

He paused for a little while and then continued, "People who have sympathy know that they have it, and people who don't just live on because it does not exist for them. It has nothing to do with being smart or powerful. It is all about your soul."

"I get what you mean," she said.

The boy said, "I think you can lose it and it certainly won't make you happy, but it will make you real." He smiled at her and said, "Don't ever lose it, Melanie."

She smiled at him and he continued, "Take Miss Martin, she lost everything. The man she loved, a beautiful lifestyle, but she is still real."

The girl looked at him and said, "John is right, you know?"

"What is that?"

"You do have a gift."

She looked at him and spoke softly, "We have had a magical summer, a summer that will define who we are for the rest of our lives. What we have learned is that you and I can never be ordinary, Conor, so let's not be ordinary about you moving away. I will not hear of it in any other way. What happens next is destiny."

She reached down and picked up her bag saying, "I have something for you."

He said with a grin, "God, don't say you have more stuff in that bag."

She laughed, and said, "It is just something for you," and she handed him a bundle tied up with a ribbon. He took it from her and saw it was a bundle of empty envelopes all addressed to her. "Just giving destiny a little helping hand," she said.

He looked at her and smiled and all he said was, "I promise."

He could see that there were tears in her eyes and she wiped them away with the back of her hand.

"So do I," she said. "Remember to write to me as soon as you get there with your address."

He nodded.

She rested her head on his shoulder again and they sat in silence. He very lightly touched her cheek with the tips of his fingers and she smiled up at him.

He said, "I expect it is time to be getting back home. My parents will think I have done a runner." He paused and looked at her saying, "And don't think that it didn't cross my mind."

As they got up from the bench, she picked up her bag and put it over her shoulder, and held her hat in her other hand. He picked up his records and the bundle of envelopes that she had given him and they started across the road towards the girl's house. He looked up at the house with its broad concrete steps and white painted columns, and the lights that twinkled inside.

"OK, Conor, this is it, number 183. You see it is written there," and she pointed to the envelopes in his hand.

She turned to him and kissed him on the cheek. She looked

at him for what seemed a long time and then said with a smile, "Conor, I am not going to say the G word, and you better not bloody say it either, or I'll drop you right there where you stand."

The two hugged each other and in an almost comical way they were half laughing and half crying. Eventually she squeezed his hand, and turned and walked up the steps of her house.

He said, "I will see you soon."

She stopped, turned around and smiled at him and then continued inside the door, closing it behind her.

Conor stood for a little while and looked at the bundle of envelopes that he had in his hand. He could get her scent from the paper and smiled to himself. He started to walk slowly in the direction of Ladbroke Grove and towards the KPH, which was just closing. The evening's events and Miss Martin's story were running around in his mind.

He walked past the KPH and crossed over to the other side of the street when he heard an argument and the sound of breaking glass. A man came flying out the door, and was set upon by another man who rained blows onto his face with his fists as he lay on the ground. The boy watched in horror at the scene as memories of 1961 came flooding back. Two more men came rushing out and pulled the two apart. After some heated debate calm was restored, and both men sheepishly shook hands and went back inside. Conor turned and started the walk up to Kensal Road. He stopped and looked at the Parish Church of St Michael. It looked very dark and gothic in the pale moonlight. As he approached the Tavistock he crossed the road, because he did not want to get caught up in another closing-time brawl.

When he reached the railway bridge, he stopped and leaned with his back to the metal walls. He could hear the usual sounds from the trains below as their motors hummed and wheels squealed against the rails. There was a figure coming up the road and Conor spotted that it was Malcolm from the Ladbroke Grove tube station. The man recognised him and said, "Hello there, Conor. Out a bit late, aren't you?"

"Yes, I was just out with some friends, and I am on my way home."

"I'd be careful out tonight as the natives are restless, if you get what I mean."

"Yes, there was a bit of agro around the KPH when I was coming up this way."

Conor noticed that the man still had his uniform on and asked, "Are you just coming off duty?"

"Yes," he said, "Someone has to keep the old transport system running."

He smiled at the boy and asked, "So tell me then?"

"Tell you what?"

"Who's the young girl that you have been hanging around with?"

The boy was taken aback and just looked at him.

"The lads in the station have been taking bets that you have gone and got yourself a girlfriend, young Conor."

The boy laughed and said, "You can tell the lads that you heard it from the horse's mouth that a girlfriend she most definitely is."

"That is great, Conor. I am going to have to be off now, or the missus will think that I've got a girlfriend too." He stopped as he was walking away and turned to the boy, "Make your way home now in case any of the revellers down there in the pub decide to make their way in this direction."

"I will Malcolm. Take care."

"Good night, Conor," said the man.

As he walked the final few yards down Kensal Road, he

wondered to himself why he did not mention to Malcolm about the move to Ireland. He thought: I am just too tired to have to go through a conversation about it. As he approached the door to the flat, he started laughing to himself when he thought of her comment: "I'll drop you where you stand." At that moment he felt a deep satisfaction from the other words she said: "You and I can never be ordinary."

Chapter 29

It was nearly six o'clock on Saturday morning, and Conor lay awake in bed with his hands behind his head. He had managed to avoid bumping into his parents the night before as he had arrived home just before they did, and went straight to bed. The teacher's story had really taken him by surprise, and he had slept very little as he thought about it. Putting a name to the anonymous man being beaten, made it more vivid and brutal, and the teacher sharing her story with them had forged a very strong bond between the three of them. He suspected that this was something that Miss Martin did not speak about often, and he felt privileged that she had shared it with them. With the teacher's story and the events of the evening spinning around in his head, he drifted off to sleep.

After about an hour of sleep, he was awakened with a bang on the door and a loud "Conor, get up" from his father. He dressed quickly and went to the kitchen where a breakfast consisting of a boiled egg with tea and toast was waiting for him. His parents were already at the table eating. He sat down and started buttering a slice of toast.

The boy's father started, "All right, then, here is the plan.

The removals van will be here at ten o'clock, and we need to have everything ready, so that we can get it all loaded and away by lunchtime. They are going to bring the van across to Dublin on the ferry, and then put the furniture into storage, so that we can collect it when we have our place sorted out. In the meantime we will stay with Aunt Lena in Kildare. We are catching the two o'clock sailing tomorrow from Holyhead, so we will need to leave at about seven tomorrow morning."

The boy was listening closely and eating at the same time. "Conor, I want you to fit pieces of cardboard to the edges of the furniture to stop them from getting chipped." He pointed to a pile of flat cardboard boxes with a knife and a roll of packing tape sitting on top. The father pointed to the other corner and there were large pieces of foam rolled up and tied with string. "I have brought the foam for us to sleep on for tonight because they will be taking the beds in the van today. Your own clothes and other small bits and pieces you can bring with you in the car tomorrow. OK, then?"

They boy nodded, finished off his breakfast and started to work.

Conor got stuck into the work and it helped to take his mind off how upset he was. Pretty soon every piece of furniture had a piece of cardboard fitted to it anywhere there was a danger of it being scratched. He even cut little triangles of cardboard which he wedged into the drawers so that they would not slide out. His father had seen him do this and nodded his approval.

Just before ten o'clock the front doorbell rang, and from the flat window the boy could see the grey roof of the removals van. His father went down to open the door and came back up the stairs with two burly men in dark blue overalls. There was a long discussion about the order of how things would be placed into the van, and when agreement was reached, the furniture started to disappear down the stairs.

Conor had chosen the few small things that he was going to take with him, and the rest he put into two large cardboard boxes to go into storage with the furniture. His satchel bag contained a few books and jotters, the LP and singles from the night before, some pens and pencils and the envelopes that Melanie had given him. He also had a duffel bag full with his clothes and shoes.

After the van had been fully loaded, there was some further discussion between the two men and the boy's father, and then the van was closed up and after a short while disappeared down Kensal Road.

The boy went into his bedroom and sat down on the foam with his head in his hands. He looked at his watch and saw that it was almost one o'clock. He thought Melanie would be finished with Miss Martin's class, having given her presentation, and would now be heading towards her home. He felt an ache in the pit of his stomach. The door of his room opened and his father came in.

He handed the boy two half-crowns and said, "Myself and your mother are going down to the pub for some lunch. Get yourself some fish and chips and a haircut." He re-emphasised, "And I mean a proper haircut."

He could hear the door closing as his parents left, and he lay back on the foam mattress. He thought: A haircut is not something I am going to get, and to hell with the consequences. He went into the kitchen and decided he would turn on the radio to hear the news. When he looked around, however, he realised it was gone in the van. He left the kitchen and moped around the flat for a little while and decided he would nip down the road and get some fish and chips, and when he came back he would pay a last visit to New York. He stopped and said to himself, "A last visit to New York," and the ache in his stomach got worse.

Eventually he made his way down the stairs and out of the flat onto Kensal Road towards Ladbroke Grove.

Conor sat on the stool in the chip shop with a mountain of cod and chips in front of him. The shop had a counter that ran all along its front window, so you could eat your food and watch the people pass by. His fish and chips were in separate greaseproof bags, and they sat on top of three large squares of newspaper. The food at the chip shop was always very good and today was no exception, but all he could do was pick at it.

Conor was on his own in the chip shop, and he could feel Guido's eyes on him. Guido was a stocky Italian man who was owner, manager and cook. He was very dark and hairy with a sweeping handlebar moustache. He spoke with a very strange accent, which at times was strongly Italian with the odd word spoken in a cockney accent. On a previous visit, Guido had told him that he was from Opera, which is a suburb of Milan. The man always spoke lovingly of his home, of sunshine, beautiful food and Barolo wine. He always painted a wonderful picture of Italy, and from listening to him over the years, he had given the boy a strong urge to visit the country.

Conor had a lot of food left over, and he carefully wrapped it up in the newspaper to take it out onto the street. Guido watched him do this and said, "Hey, ragazzo, what for you no eat your food?" The chip shop owner always took personal offence to anyone who did not finish their food. Over the years the boy had even seen people told to get out and never come back over this.

He turned to the man and said, "I am going to have this at home."

"OK, is good no?"

"It is the very best, Guido."

The man smiled broadly.

As the boy was going through the door he turned and said, "See you, Guido."

"Addio, bello," came the reply in a strong Italian accent.

When he was sure that he was well out of view, he placed the food into the nearest bin and strolled back towards Kensal Road.

On his way up the street, he passed the Tavistock Pub and as always on the weekends it was very busy. Most of the customers were the same Irish builders that he had seen the evening before on his way up Ladbroke Grove to Miss Martin's flat. He did not look in, but just strolled past on the pavement. As he had just passed the pub, he felt a hand on the sleeve of his jacket and he was marched up the street. The boy turned and he saw that it was his father. There was a strong smell of drink and he knew exactly what was coming. They veered off the road into the small bright red building that was Ken's barber shop. The shop was empty apart from Ken himself who was standing looking out of the window.

Conor despised Ken the barber. He always got the feeling that the man took great pleasure in cutting his hair off, knowing that this made the boy unhappy. He was a very small, thin man with sleek jet-black hair and a pencil moustache. He greeted them as they entered, "How are you, Pat. For the two of you, is it?"

"No Ken, just the young lad, short back and sides."

The father guided the boy onto the leather swivel chair in front of the mirror and the barber swept a black nylon sheet across the boy's shoulders and tied it at the back of his neck.

He caught the boy's hair in his hand and turned to the father said, "I am going to have to charge you time and material here, Pat."

The barber pumped up the chair with the silver foot pedal

until the boy's head was centred in the mirror. He then took a silver scissors out of his top pocket and started to hack away at the boys long black hair. The locks of hair fell onto the boy's shoulders and then to the ground around the base of the chair. Conor just stared ahead at himself in the mirror. The barber turned to the boy's father and said, "Someone was telling me that you were going back to Ireland, Pat."

"Yes, tomorrow," said the father.

"What's happening over there, then?"

The father looked at the barber and said, "There are great opportunities now in Ireland with its new industries and businesses. It is not like when I left it after the war."

The barber said, "There is nothing I like more than a good pint of Guinness, Pat."

"Did you know," said the boy's father, "that it tastes completely different over there – much creamier."

"I did not know that. I must visit Ireland someday," said the barber.

The father said, "Anyway, I am going back to finish my pint. How much is that I owe you?"

"That will be one and six, Pat."

"OK then, there's two schillings. Make sure that he looks right," and he handed the coin to the man.

The barber responded, "Good man, Pat, badly needed."

The boy could see the smile on the barber's face, but he thought it was more of amusement than gratitude.

When the father had left, the barber said, "He is a great man, isn't he?"

The boy knew from the man's tone that he was trying to get a reaction from him, but he refused to be drawn out so he said nothing.

He could see that this unsettled the barber a little. The barber then tried some further conversation, "You must be looking forward to going home then."

Again the boy made no response to this.

He could see that it bothered the man that he could not elicit a response. As he reached for the electric hair clippers to trim the hairs on the back of the boy's neck, he just muttered something to himself under his breath and started the clippers.

When he had finished, he lifted off the black nylon sheet and with a small, soft brush swept the loose hairs off the boy's neck and shoulders.

"There you go," said the man, "ready for home."

Again there was no comment from the boy. He just got off the chair and looked at the man as he brushed himself down.

The barber called out to the boy as he walked towards the door, "Good luck, then. Tell them all over there that Ken said hello."

The boy just stopped in the doorway. He turned and stared at the barber and then went out the door onto the street without a word.

As he walked up the road, he thought to himself: There is one little man that I won't miss.

Chapter 30

Conor went directly into the Portobello when he got back, and straight out the door onto Bleecker Street. It was a very hot day in New York and he took off his jacket and flung it over his shoulder. He made straight for the square, and as he walked, his anger about the haircut subsided. He thought to himself: I am really going to miss all of this. As he crossed into the square, he looked towards the arch and saw John sitting in his usual spot. He waved his arm over his head and John waved back to him. As he approached, John looked at him and said, "What the fuck happened to you?"

The boy looked at him and said, "It is OK, John, I told them nothing."

They both laughed out loud.

The man pointed to the boy's head and said, "By parental order, I expect."

"You don't think I would willingly do this, do you?"

The boy could see that the man looked a lot better and as he sat down he said, "You look good."

"Yeah, they were able to patch me up a bit. I feel a lot better."

John looked at him and said, "Tony, at The Preacher, told me you are heading home."

"Yes, I go tomorrow."

"I will be sorry to see you go. It has been a great summer."

Conor looked at him and said, "Thanks, John, but me heading home is a bit more complicated."

"How so?"

"We are moving to Ireland," said the boy.

"So, do you not like that?"

The boy just looked at him.

Suddenly it dawned on the man, and he said, "Oh God, I forgot about the girl."

"Yes, she is in London," the boy said as he looked down at his shoes.

"That must be painful."

"You have no fucking idea," said the boy. "We spoke about it, and Melanie thinks that we have both changed somehow this summer, and our experiences will define who we are for the rest of our lives, and the rest is destiny. She said we cannot ever be ordinary."

"What do you think?" asked the man.

Conor thought for a little while and said, "I think she is right, and our lives will be defined by the moments we have shared this summer. It doesn't make it hurt less though."

The man looked out towards the fountain in the centre of the square, and then turned back to look at the boy and said, "Having met the young lady, my money is on you two."

"Thanks, John. That is good to hear."

The boy smiled to himself, and asked, "Do you know what she said to me?"

"What?" said the man.

"She said if I said goodbye to her, she would drop me right there where I stand."

They both laughed, "I believe she would too," the man said.

"She is right, you know, you two will never be ordinary."

They sat in silence for a while and John said, "Come on, Conor, let's go to The Preacher and I will buy you a cup of coffee."

They got up and started across the square, "You know the new hair look is starting to grow on me."

"Are you serious?" the boy said.

"No," said the man, "it looks stupid."

They sat in The Preacher sipping two mugs of coffee. Tony had greeted them when they came in, but he was busy dealing with deliveries and said he would join them when he got a chance.

They sat in silence for a while, and then John looked at the boy and said, "You are a mystery my young friend. There is much more going on with you than you say."

"I do have secrets, yes."

He knew that the man saw beyond what was said – but he never asked questions.

"It is funny," said the boy, "although you never try to influence me, I have learned so much from you this summer."

"It is all within yourself, Conor. I told you before, your perception is unique."

John lit a cigarette and stirring his coffee, he asked the boy, "So the girl aside, how do you think living in Ireland is going to be for you?"

"I don't know. I have been there many times during the summer, but living there is going to be different, I expect." He looked at the man and said, "You know they teach the Irish language in school?"

"Knowing another language can't be a bad thing, can it?"

"No, but anywhere I have gone in Ireland, they don't speak it."

The man frowned and said, "That does not seem to make too much sense."

The boy took a sip of his coffee and said, "My parents are really looking forward to moving home. It is something they have dreamt of since they moved to London in the forties."

He looked at the man and said, "I don't see Ireland as they do."

"How do they see it?"

"They see it in a romantic way. It is their home, their identity."

They were silent for a little while.

The boy said, "Being Irish is their identity, not mine."

"What is your identity?"

"I am me. I am not Irish. I am not English."

The man smiled. "How do you think other people see your identity?"

"That is a very good question." The boy thought about it for a while. "In England they would define me as Irish, because my parents are Irish, and in Ireland they would define me as English irrespective of my parents. When I have been in Ireland I sometimes get the sense that I am disliked because of my accent, so I have learned to speak very little."

The man sighed and leaned forward with his elbows on the table and said, "There is a dark history between Ireland and England that goes back centuries." He looked at the boy and said, "The pages of Irish history are filled with a number of struggles for independence. Britain has never been compassionate about threats against the empire, so these uprisings were dealt with swiftly and brutally. The consequence of this history is an ingrained mistrust of England and the British Empire by many of the Irish people."

The boy looked down at his coffee and said, "I have heard

of that. My father often speaks about the potato famine in the nineteenth century, and the Easter Rising of 1916."

The man nodded. "I have some Irish friends that have lived here in New York for forty years and they still speak of England coldly."

They sipped some more coffee and John put out his cigarette into the ashtray and continued, "I know a little of the history of Ireland. The War of Independence against Britain was truly heroic, and the leaders were scholars and visionaries not soldiers. But when independence was eventually achieved, it was not for the entire Island of Ireland, and the north remained part of the United Kingdom. The treaty that was signed created two separate countries, Northern Ireland and the Irish Free State — now known as the Republic of Ireland. This split the country into two factions, pro-treaty and anti-treaty and resulted in a bloody and bitter civil war. In some cases, similar to the American Civil War, this literally pitted brother against brother. Although the fighting stopped in 1922, the Civil War lives on from a political perspective to this day."

He paused for a little while and said, "I have noticed that my Irish friends here in New York often speak of the War of Independence, but never of the Civil War."

"Why do you think that is?" asked the boy.

John thought about this for a little while and said, "I expect there is comfort in having a common enemy."

They sat quietly for a while and the man said, "So, I don't expect you will be visiting here next summer then?"

"I don't know. I think it will be difficult." He looked at the man and smiled, "But I didn't think I would be here this year, and yet here I am."

John smiled back at him. "Good man. I would love to hear all about your exploits in Ireland." And with that he reached into his green khaki bag and handed him a notebook with a black leather cover. It was just the right size to fit into the pocket of a pants or a jacket. Along with the notebook, he gave him a beautiful black fountain pen.

"These are for you, so that you can take some notes as you go."

"Thank you," Conor said, "for everything," and he put the notebook and pen into the top pocket of his jacket.

As they were sitting quietly, Tony came over with a tray that contained some more coffee and a glass of Jack Daniels. He placed the whiskey in front of John, and the coffees in front of himself and the boy, and sat down.

"So are we celebrating or mourning Conor's leaving? What is the story, men?"

"I think a bit of both, Tony," said Conor.

Tony looked at the boy and said, "Let me guess – girl trouble."

The boy smiled and said, "You are not wrong."

Tony looked at John and said, "You know I had Kathy here with me yesterday and this guy came in, and she wouldn't stop talking about him for the rest of the day."

The three laughed and Tony said as he looked at the boy, "I think you are a bit of a heartbreaker, young Conor." He then looked at the boy's hair and said, "But I am not sure now though, seeing as you have decided to go and join the Marine Corps."

Again the three laughed.

Tony said, "Well with regards to your girl problem, you are talking to two of the most unsuccessful men in the love department that have ever walked the earth. So with that said we have nothing of any value to contribute."

He held up his mug and they joined him as he toasted, "Here's to Conor and the love of his life," and they said cheers.

They sat and chatted for a while. Tony had that sense of fun and humour that lifted the spirits of all around him. The boy found that for a half an hour or so, he forgot all about his troubles, and then Tony headed back to mind the bar. After a while John turned to him and said, "OK then, Conor, it is time to make tracks." And with that they left The Preacher. Conor shook hands with Tony, who told him he would not let him go until he promised to come back next year. Eventually the boy promised and the man and boy left the bar and went out into the bright sunshine of Bleecker Street.

The two stood outside on the sidewalk, and John held out his hand, "If you say the goodbye word, just like your beautiful young friend, I will also drop you where you stand."

The boy smiled at him and said, "I will see you again soon."

They shook hands and walked off in different directions. Without turning around the man just said, "Hasta luego."

Chapter 31

After leaving John at The Preacher, Conor walked back into the Portobello and locked the door behind him, putting the key into his pocket. He closed down the door on the stage and took out the sweeping brush and swept both the stage and the pub. He cleaned down the bar and got out the brass polish, and buffed up all of the brass fittings. The place was spotless, but he still polished the table and chairs with furniture polish until they shone. He reached behind the stage curtain and took out the small canvas bag. Into this he placed the key of the door to Bleecker Street alongside the little oil can and the torch. Taking the book of matches from his pocket, he lit what was left of the candle in the wine bottle and jumped down off the stage. He crossed the floor and sat up onto the bar counter looking back at the stage. It was a magical scene, and the memories of the times he had spent here came flooding back to him.

He saw the eight-year-old boy pulling down the beer crates row by row and opening up the big red velvet curtain. He saw the terrified boy running out of the pub after his first visit to New York. He saw Melanie's beautiful smile when she first saw the place. He saw the boy, the girl and the writer sitting at the table having their lunch. He felt cold and miserable at the thought of leaving all of it behind. This was his sanctuary and his fortress and there were only two people that he had shared it with, the man from California that had become his friend and mentor, and a beautiful girl whose spirit had shone a light into his life. He wanted to wait a while here because this image was all that he would carry with him for a long, long, time. He thought of Miss Martin and her sad story, and of Matthew who paid the price for the right to sing. He sighed and asked himself what it all meant, but he had no answer.

He sat for a long time, and his thoughts drifted off to New York. He thought of the Wang family and how close they were to John. He smiled to himself when he thought that when you become a friend of the writer you are a friend for life. But he bet that if you are an enemy to the man you had better be very careful. He thought of Tony and his daughter Kathy and how much he liked The Preacher. As all of these characters floated around in his head, he imagined a big party here in the Portobello. He saw all of them on the stage, sitting at tables talking and laughing. The Wang's would have brought food and Tony would have brought the drinks. His Aunt Claire and John would be in deep discussion, and Tony would be telling stories of Greenwich Village. Conor himself would be sitting and talking with Melanie. All of these figures were swirling in front of him on the stage. Then the stage cleared and he saw Miss Martin alone on the stage with a great look of sadness on her face. Her look reminded him of the lady in the painting *American Gothic*. Then all of the images disappeared and he sat looking at the empty stage with its table and candle, still beautiful, but empty.

As he sat on the bar, he realised that apart from the trips to Ireland, he had spent time every single day of his life here since he was eight years old. He knew that nothing he would experience in Ireland could match the magic of the Portobello. It was a beautiful and noble place that was his alone. It had been his refuge and his friend, with all its wonderful secrets that it kept hidden underneath the stage. The emotion had been building deep within him for days. He had fought hard against it — but now it came out of him in great sobs. As he sobbed he jumped down off the counter and leapt up onto the stage, dancing crazily around in a circle. He stopped in the middle and looked across at the bar. He stared at the bar for a long time, as he wanted to imprint this image into his mind also, so that he could see it when he was away from here.

He stood in the middle of the stage and said out loud:

Ghosts of war and of peace.
Ghosts of love and of hate
Ghosts of nothingness.
Ghosts of sympathy.
Thank you for your company.

He was silent then and was no longer crying. Looking straight ahead of him he took a deep bow. He held the bow for a while and then straightened himself.

Eventually he blew the candle out and fixed the three chairs neatly around the table. He climbed down from the stage and carefully pulled down on the rope at the side and closed the curtain. He had placed his little canvas bag on the bar counter, and into it he put the notebook and pen that John had given him along with the book of matches from The Preacher. With the bag in his hand, he left the Portobello behind him and went upstairs into the flat.

*

SONGS *and* PORTOBELLOS

It was Sunday morning and the boy was sitting in the back of his father's old Ford with his mother in the front passenger seat. All around them were bags, and the boot was full of bedclothes and suitcases. Behind the car and on the roof of the house where the Tomasevskis had lived, stood Christopher the white pigeon with the small brown flecks on its wings. The bird was standing very still looking down on the street.

His father came out of the flat, and threw his key back into the letterbox. He got in behind the wheel of the car, and turned to ask the boy, "Did you leave your keys in the flat?"

Feeling the keys in his trouser pocket, the boy said, "Yes."

"All right, then," said the father, "off we go," and he started the car and they headed down Kensal Road.

Conor stared straight ahead and did not look behind him as they drove away.

Acknowledgements

To Tony for the drawing board and T-square.
To Mary for the bright red bicycle.
To Matt for the tenner and the loan of your boots.